Ré Ó Laighléis

TERROR
ON THE BURREN

[signature: Ré Ó Laighléis]

MÓINÍN

First published in Irish 1995 by
Cló Iar-Chonnachta

This edition published 1998 by MÓINÍN,
Ballyvaughan, Co. Clare, Ireland

First print 1998

The author asserts the moral right to be identified
as the author of this work

A CIP catalogue record for this book is available
from the British Library

ISBN 0 9532777 0 4

Printed and bound in Ireland by
Colour Books, Dublin

Set in Palatino 11.5/15

Cover design by Alanna Corballis
Edited and typeset by Carole Devaney

Born in 1953, Ré Ó Laighléis is a native of Sallynoggin, Co. Dublin. A graduate of the University of Galway (1978), he has taken postgraduate degrees in education from St. Patrick's College, Dublin, and from Boston College, Massachusetts, where he is registered as a Consultant Reading Specialist. He taught in Galway for twelve years.

Since 1992, Ó Laighléis has been a full-time writer and lives in the Burren, Co. Clare. He is a well-known dramatist, working particularly in children's drama. Six of his plays were awarded the All Ireland Schools Drama title and he is a three-times winner of the Aodh Ó Ruairc Commemorative Drama Award. His definitive work in drama, *Aistear Intinne* (COISCÉIM, 1996), is written for teachers and children.

Ó Laighléis is best known, however, as a writer of novels and short stories. He is published in English and Italian, and is the biggest selling contemporary writer in the Irish language. He writes for both the adult and teenage reader, and has been awarded numerous Oireachtas literary awards in the various genres. He is twice winner of The Bisto Book of the Year Merit Award. On the international front, he is the recipient of the 1995 NAMLLA Award (North American Minority Languages Literary Award) and the 1997 White Ravens Literary Award.

Terror on the Burren, in its original form, was the winner of the Seán Ó hÉigeartaigh Commemorative Award, the Bisto Book of the Year Merit Award and was Ó Laighléis's second work to be nominated for *The Irish Times* Literary Awards.

With thanks & love to
my father and mother, Kevin and Josephine,
and to my friends and fellow-lovers of
the Burren, Bernie & Doreen Comyn,
Valerie Bowe, Paul Carter & Janet Temple,
Jim Connors, Rick & Marcia Considine,
Jack Gilligan, Frank Golden, Ian Kirkham
& Judith Ross Kirkham, Brendan &
Catherine O'Donoghue, Heather Parsons,
my uncle Bill Proctor, Paul & Kay Russell,
Manus Walsh, and 'the terrible trio'
Carole, Melanie & Fidelma.

A special thanks to Jonathan Williams.

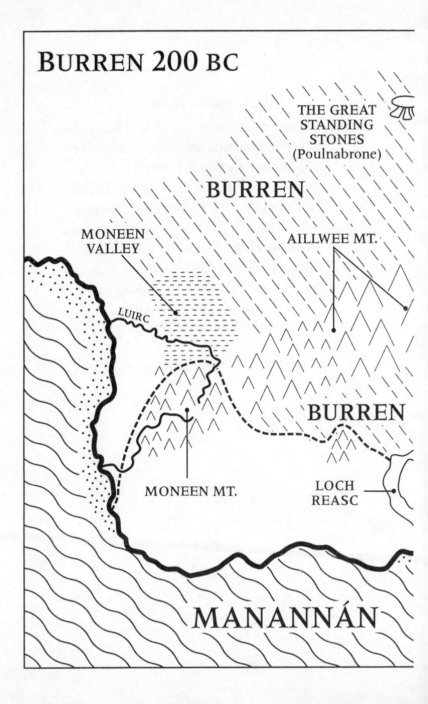

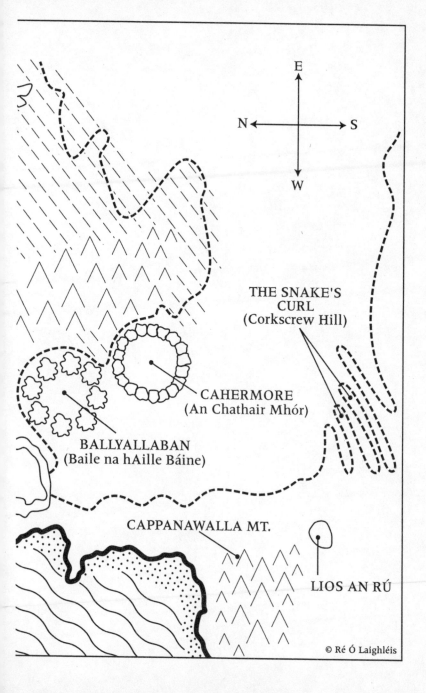

A Note on Place Names

All places depicted in *Terror on the Burren* are extant. In cases such as The Great Standing Stones (present-day Poulnabrone) and The Snake's Curl (present-day Corkscrew Hill), names have been devised to reflect the physical nature of the feature in question while, at the same time, endeavouring linguistically to accommodate the notion of 'time past' and to sustain the general flavour of the text.

Names of townlands (such as Loch Reasc and Ballyallaban), of mountains (such as Moneen, Aillwee and Cappanawalla) and of ancient settlements (such as Cahermore, Ballyallaban and Lios an Rú) are given here as they are used in the present-day parlance of the people of the Burren.

The Gleninsheen Collar takes its name from the townland in which it was retrieved. In 1932 Paddy Nolan, a local farmer found the collar wedged in a gryke (deep crevice) in the Burren's limestone surface. Highly ornamental, it was fashioned in gold in the Late Bronze Age (*circa* 700 BC). It is one of Ireland's most treasured artifacts and is now housed in the National Museum, Dublin.

The habitation sites of Ballyallaban and Cahermore are but two of many such sites throughout the Burren. They are, respectively, perfect examples of the earthen and stone forts built throughout the country. As is depicted in the novel, each type has an eye to defence, the inner habitation area being encircled by a high earthen bank, often tree-lined (as in Ballyallaban), outside of which is a deep moat, or by a high, deep and solidly constructed stone wall (as in Cahermore), outside of which there is a sheer drop of some twelve to twenty feet. As excavation of these sites has not occurred and there is evidence of their existence in ancient manuscripts, the author has taken the liberty of having them *in situ* at the time in which *Terror on the Burren* is set.

The Coming

It is the year 200 BC. The ocean, not yet named, is angry. For days now, it has rolled and swollen, stirring the depths of its blackness and churning the currents upwards to catch the silver of the sun. There is no rest for waters such as these, for, to the east there is little and to the west there is even less. These are the waters that go far and yet go nowhere. These are the waters of Time and of Timelessness.

A boat, no, a raft of sorts, is thrown up on the wave. Clinging to its mast, the ravaged figures of five, six maybe — yes, six — submit their being to the hands of Manannán, the Merciful and the Merciless, God of all the Seas. His will *will* be done.

A crack! And suddenly, the mast is broken, crashing down on to Relco's leg. Immediately, his eldest son, Emlik, is at his father's side, shielding him from the searing winds that have, for weeks now, made gritty redness of their faces. The flittered, windblown ribbons of their sail, desperately clinging to the half-mast and working hard to bolster Manannán's ferocity against them, tear hard into Emlik's face, as he tries to ease his father's pain. The upper half of the broken mast has not fully detached itself and Emlik finds it impossible to remove the stubborn beam without help.

"Break off the mast, break off the mast," Emlik frantically shouts to his brother, Darkon. His words, taken on the wind's wings, are hastened to some far and long-lost corner of the world. Darkon has not heard and still he huddles to his mother, Alyana, and his younger sisters, Raithnika and Frayika. The quartet has formed a strong, defensive chain against the elements, each fixing their right arm around another's waist, and using the left to hold firmly on to what has now become a half-mast.

"Get up, Darkon, get up and release the broken mast."

Though Emlik's words are again whipped afar to quarters never known, there is no mistaking the gestures which accompany them. Raithnika, the older of the sisters, has seen these gestures and knows, as does Darkon, the message that Emlik is imparting. Darkon still does not move until Raithnika breaks the chain and gestures to him to do likewise. With obvious reluctance, Darkon does as he is bade, and Raithnika, standing now and clinging single-handedly to the upright part of the mast, ensures the safety of her mother and of Frayika by indicating to them to place both hands on the mast.

The two halves of the mast are held together only by a sliver, a sinew of wood. Emlik, with his left arm around his father, uses the right to lever the wooden beam off the broken leg, while Darkon and Raithnika push outwards at their end. With little effort, the broken upright comes away, hurtles out onto the rolling swell and, in a matter of seconds, is as far away from them as is their memory of the last time they have eaten.

Emlik looks towards the two, still standing in the centre of the raft. Raithnika smiles, a caring smile. She is tall, blue-eyed and blonde, just like Emlik. Their bond is one of constance. She sits, and Emlik's gaze shifts to the eyes of his younger brother. Darkon stands, looking hard with his black eyes into his brother's face, knowing that only a few short minutes earlier, the darkness of his nature had revealed itself. He slithers down the half-mast and the huddle that had been their shield against the storm reforms itself. And the will of Manannán, Lord of the Open Seas, persists.

The sun burns hard in the blueness of the sky. Nothing that endures its gaze for long can speak of comfort. As his eyes slowly, painfully open, Emlik does not realise that it is his own hand that rests across his forehead, shielding him from the blazing sun. Time in such matters cannot be gauged. It may be a night, or many nights, or even the space of one full moon that he is lying here. There is no way to tell, and so, it matters little. For some moments, he remains still, making sense of the itching that he feels against his skin. Then, as if grasping at a nettle, he clenches his left hand, which has been resting palm-down by his side, and tightly seizes some of the irritants. He raises the hand to his eyes and sees that it is filled with sandy coral. He is on dry land.

Emlik rolls on to his side and slowly, gently, raises himself, feeling throughout his efforts the pain that speaks of doing battle with one far greater than himself. He looks then to the ocean. White gulls now sit on the serenity of its greenness, undulating softly with the waves. It has fought and won, and now it rests, for forever there will be battle to be done, and only the warrior who knows the art of peace can fully know the art of war.

Where are the others, Emlik wonders. He looks to both sides, along the huge expanse of sand on to which he has been thrown. To the south the sun is blinding, negating his best efforts to make sense of what he is observing. It is better when he looks north. In the distance, he sees a small and huddled mound that is neither earth nor rock. He moves quickly towards it and, as he moves, he fights his under-standing of what this mound may be. His heart and feet quicken with each other and soon he is near enough to see the white fleece clothing that is Relco's mark. He moves now, even more quickly, and reaches the point where his father lies. Emlik turns the body on its back; in his chest, two holes, five or six inches apart, have been made, draining life's blood from him.

Frantically, he shakes his father, telling him they

have survived the wrath of Manannán; there are other battles to fight. Then, knowing that all fights to come will be watched over only by the spirit of Relco, the tears of this first son, Emlik, fall from his face on to his father's. Emlik rubs the wetness into his father's cheeks and knows within that for all the years to come, he must bear his father's honour. He feels his heart tighten and he knows the pain of loss.

"Emlik, Emlik!" The voice is far off. Emlik turns back towards the sun again, but it blinds him as before.

"Emlik, Emlik!" It is coming from the hill beyond the sand. He turns to face the dunes, which dare, in times of anger, to stem great Manannán's huge tides.

"Emlik! Over here, Emlik!" The forms of Raithnika and Frayika dance and wave to him from the level land that tops the dunes.

Emlik is suddenly fired with energy and excitement. He scales the dune with an alacrity defiant of all they have gone through, reaches his sisters and his mother (whom he had not seen when at the level of the sea). They stand in conclave, arms tightly around one another, braced against the world.

After some moments like this Emlik speaks, quite soberly.

"Father is dead," he says.

They hang their heads, wanting to cry, but finding that even the energy to release their pain has been stolen from them. Their sorrow flows inwards and is of silence; the most painful of the sorrows, for its journey to rest is then doubled.

"He has been gored by some wild creature," Emlik says. His directness is intended to tear the others from their grieving.

"We must do what is demanded of us."

"What of Darkon?" asks Alyana.

"I have seen nothing of him. And you?"

"No, he has not been with us," answers Frayika. "Perhaps he has been swept further to the north."

"Perhaps. We will see in time," says Emlik.

There was no love of son or brother when they spoke of Darkon. He was different to the others. He was older than the girls and second only to Emlik. It was said that when he was born, a black cloud crossed the path of the sun and all was cold and dark for a time not measured. This, it was said, was the cause of blackness in his hair and in his eyes. And it was much in their belief that the eyes, above all else, reflected the inner self.

Darkon seemed pained when he looked upon his brother, Emlik. They were not at one. As a boy, Emlik had trained his younger brother in the art of hunting, of shooting arrows, of spearing fish, and these, he told him, were the greater elements of the Art of Caring. There was a reason to this art and it was in the reason, not in the act itself, that the nobility of Caring did abide. Darkon had no need of reason and neither had he need of caring. All things, for him, were of the act, and so, the arts of hunting, of shooting arrows and of spearing fish were of the kill, and that was all.

By the time darkness had chased the sun below the waves and to another world, they were ready. Frayika and her mother, Alyana, had spent much time heaping stones that were, just like themselves, swept in on the waves. They had made a cairn, a mound of stones, and now all four were topping it with wood, which earlier Raithnika and Emlik had gathered for the burning. It was good that much of the wood that was gathered was of themselves and of their father, Relco, for it happened in their search that they came upon many of the wooden beams from which their raft had been constructed.

When this was done, Alyana and her daughters put sand into the wounds in Relco's chest. It was important that, when leaving this world, he would be whole, just as he had been whole when he came into it. Emlik then took his father's body, mounted the cairn and laid it out, face upwards, on the wood, spreading the arms and legs so that they pointed to the corners of the earth. Then, each taking a lighted torch from the blaze that Emlik had made earlier, they inserted them into the ends and sides of the wooden pyre. The fire burned with great ferocity, casting its light far into the night, making little of the darkness. Behind the pyre, far off on the dune where earlier the women had been found, Emlik could see a figure shimmer in the waves of heat. He moved away from the pyre, dismissing the distortion that the dancing heatwaves made and saw, in the light of Relco's fire, a big black poc goat. The goat stood bold and daring and bent its head to show its horns, the tips of which glistened when the light of the fire caught their redness.

Emlik looked hard; despite the distance, their eyes met, and the poc goat bleated a message of foreboding, then turned and disappeared into the darkness of the night. Shaken within by a sense of evil, Emlik kept his peace and bent his head at his father's burning.

2

Danger and a New Place to live

Time passed. The sun had set many times since they had made their camp down by a stream, just beyond the dunes. Here, they were sheltered from the cutting winds that would, when times were angry, sweep in from the sea. There was fresh and running water from the mountain stream in which they could bathe themselves and wash the skins of the dead animals Emlik would carry back each day.

Emlik, like his father, was a great hunter. Early each morning, he would leave the camp, making sure before he'd go that his mother and his sisters were safe and provided for. He went high into the mountain rock, which by day formed a hard grey shield against the world beyond and, by night, a dark blue curtain, sheltering them from the cold north winds.

While Emlik was away, the women gathered sticks and set a fire. The huge bronze cauldron which they had brought with them and which had miraculously survived the rolling of the seas, was now in constant use. In it, Alyana would boil the skins of the animals, stirring to soften the hides and release any flesh that may have survived the cut. Then Frayika, using the

large and many-toothed comb which Emlik had
fashioned from a thighbone, found one day on the
mountainside, would score the hide from top to
bottom and then from side to side. This, it was
believed in the Nordic lands from which they had
come, freed evils of the animal from the skin and drew
them to the Otherworld. Frayika then coated the
scored hide with sea sand, letting its caustic saline mix
purge any lurking impurities not yet released.

Raithnika, the older of the sisters, together with
her brother, Emlik, was now joint leader of this family.
Her mother, though uninjured in their crossing of the
ocean, was without spirit. Relco, Alyana's husband of
many years, had been called to *Valhalla*, final resting
place of the great warriors, and with him, her spirit
too had left her. And so, it befell Raithnika to fill her
mother's role.

In their division of labour Raithnika was the maker
of things. She would take the skins which Frayika had
scored and sanded and rewash them, returning the
dead impurities in the sand back into the earth. After
hanging them to dry, absorbing the heat of the sun
and of the limestone hill, she would shape them into
clothing or coverings for their huts.

It was such a day, as the women worked the skins,
that they heard the excited call of Emlik in the distance. Immediately, they left aside their tasks and
rushed forward to the brow of the bank above the
stream. Standing together, their eyes scanned the
greyness of the rugged mountain before them. They

felt their hearts beat at the thought of oncoming danger. All the time they could hear the nearing call of Emlik, growing in excitement. Then Frayika, who had the sharpest vision of the three, saw the distant figure bobbing up and down as he crossed the limestone scree that had been rejected by the mountain.

"It's Emlik, see," Frayika said, pointing to where she had spotted him.

Alyana and Raithnika followed the direction in which she pointed and saw Emlik making for the camp in great haste.

"He is being followed. There is an animal chasing him," shouted Alyana in alarm.

Raithnika came further forward and could see that Alyana was right. Behind her brother, giving chase, was a low-sized, burly animal of a kind that they had never seen before.

"Quickly, Mother, back to the camp!" Raithnika cried, ushering her mother towards their settlement again. "Frayika, get the spears."

Frayika moved rapidly and was quickly by Raithnika's side again, bearing with her two long wooden shafts on which were mounted hard and sharpened flints.

"Stay here, Mother," Raithnika ordered once again. "Frayika, come." The sisters crossed the stream and moved with speed in the direction of the oncoming danger. Their hearts beat fast and they could feel the earth rumble beneath their running feet as, all the time, their brother Emlik, pursued now even closer by this wild thing, came nearer to them.

"Go back, go back," Emlik shouted in desperation. For the first time, they could make sense of Emlik's cries. By now, however, it was too late for them to think of turning back. Besides, their brother was in danger and it was not so long ago since he had saved them from even greater peril. They stood fast. They could see, though they did not know its kind, a wild boar, brown and black in colour, gaining on their brother. Emlik's broken spear jutted from its neck and blood flowed from the animal.

"Get down, get down," Emlik shouted frantically, as he rushed on towards them. "He will kill you. Get down!"

The sisters looked at each other. There was an unspoken bond between them and they knew what they must do. Emlik now was only yards away and half as far again came the trundling animal. The sisters stood firm. They had, at times, seen Emlik, and their father before him, in such danger. They knew what must be done and hoped that they could do it. As Emlik surged through the space between them, they saw the viciousness of the onrushing beast.

"Now," cried Raithnika, and at one and the same time, they summoned all their might and released their spears. The spearheads met their target and, side by side, entered the forehead of the boar, halting him immediately in his chase, bringing his burly body crashing to the ground. He shrieked, a piercing shriek, and groaned, then made to get to his feet again. The girls, now stunned and immobilised by what they had managed to do, looked on at the animal, with all three spears now hanging from him, as he found his feet and heaved his body, preparing himself for a final effort. He bared his teeth and grunted loudly. His eyes, red with anger, were watering with rage. He scratched the ground before him with one hoof and leaned forward, readying himself for attack. Once, twice, three times he scratched. The girls cringed beneath his gaze. Then, when it seemed the sisters were at the mercy of this beast, Emlik lunged forward again in fury and hurled a rock, striking him between the eyes. The boar stood motionless for some seconds, eyes fixed straight ahead, and then, emitting one long and yielding cry, toppled over, dead.

The sisters and their brother fell down on their knees and knew that, in their time of need, the spirit of Relco had watched over them.

Later that evening, as they sat around the fire watching the one-time dangerous beast roasting on the spit, Emlik related how earlier that day, he had come upon the animal and, better still, how he had found an idyllic place for them to live.

"I was halfway down the other side of the mountain," he said, "when, in the distance, I saw this beautiful green area pressed between two high places. I kept it in my mind's eye even after coming off the mountain, crossing many streams and stones, making for the place."

"Well, did you reach it?" asked Frayika, somewhat

impatiently. Her eagerness betrayed the question that was also in Alyana's and Raithnika's minds.

"Wait, let me finish my story," said Emlik, as, when he saw her enthusiasm for what he had to tell, he decided to prolong the suspense, believing in his heart that this would sweeten the telling all the more.

"As I neared the place, I heard voices."

"Voices! People!" Raithnika interjected. "There are others here then?"

"Yes, there are others. I heard voices and I approached the green place with great caution. There were bushes nearby and I hid behind them, looking on."

"Is it their settlement?" Alyana asked, somewhat abruptly, tiring a little of the teasing way in which her son was sharing his news with them. Emlik could detect her annoyance and, out of respect for her, he decided to hurry up the telling.

"No, Mother, they do not live there."

The womenfolk looked at one another, heartened by the news and hopeful that this place that Emlik had come upon could possibly be theirs.

"They were there hunting the animal," he said.

"The one that chased you?"

"Yes, except that there were many of them — five or six hands times," he said, indicating a number between twenty-five and thirty.

"How many of the humans?" asked Frayika.

"Four, maybe five — no more than that. They had killed two of the animals and had tied and mounted

them on staffs. They were moving away when I
arrived and so I waited until they had gone some
distance from the place before I left the bushes."

"Tell us of the place itself," Raithnika urged.

"Well, I cannot tell much, except that it looks very
green and fertile. As I left the bushes, I stood on a
sharp, crisp twig and it snapped, alerting our friend
here," said Emlik, pointing towards the roasting boar.

"So, you took to your heels, huh!"

"Exactly, Frayika."

They all laughed. It was laughter of relief; relief
that, after the dangers of the day, they were still a family, seated safely around their campfire and planning
what they might do.

"This place — is it far?" Alyana asked. On this
particular evening Alyana showed much more
interest than she had shown at any time since Relco's
death. Perhaps the near loss of her son and of her
daughters earlier that day jolted her from the shock
that had come over her when her husband died.

"No more than four thousand paces, and that is
going around the mountain," Emlik responded.

"And water? Is there water nearby?" asked
Frayika.

"Yes. Yes, a stream, as fresh and as pure as we have
here," replied Emlik.

"We will go there," Alyana said. "We will make a
new beginning and your father's spirit will be happy
that we have carried out his wish that we should have
a peaceful place to live."

Next morning, while the sun still sat low in the eastern sky, they assembled all their goods. Raithnika had made back packs of the bigger skins and into these they placed their many bone, bronze and stone implements of work. They spent much time pondering how they might take the large bronze cauldron to the new place. It had travelled many miles with them and had been made by their father's hands. It was also important in their work, but it was too large and far too heavy to take with them without the aid of transport. Emlik suggested that they hide it in the dunes and that he would return again when they had found a way of moving it. They pulled it the short distance to the back of the dunes and mounted stones around it, concealing it from view.

The sun was higher in the sky now and its heat was welcome. They crossed the stream that had served them well since they had come to this place and then, turning back to face it again, they each threw a stone into the water and watched them come to rest on the sandy bed. It was their custom that one must always leave one's mark in gratitude where one has been served by Nature. Emlik then led them to the south and they followed in single file, with Raithnika to the rear.

Emlik was seventeen summers now, one more than his brother, Darkon, of whom they had still heard nothing. Being the eldest, it was his duty to lead. He was tall and sturdy, fair of skin and even fairer still of hair. His muscular arms and legs suggested strength and agility far beyond his years. His mind too was that of someone older, wiser, more mature than others of his age. Even before his father had died, the others often looked to him for wisdom, for decision. All, that is, except Darkon.

Raithnika too, like her brother, Emlik, was strong and wise. She was one and one-half summers younger than Darkon and was very beautiful. Just as Emlik had, in childhood, trained Darkon in the Art of Caring, so too Raithnika had trained her younger sister. It was she who showed Frayika how to clean and score the skins, how to make beads of coral and of bone, how to cook and, above all else, how to respect the elements and the Earth upon whose mercy they relied.

"Let's rest a little now," Frayika said, easing the load from her back as she spoke.

"Yes, why not! We have come quite some way already," Emlik agreed.

By now the sun, which was near its highest point, had moved much further to the south. They sat and looked back towards the place from which they had journeyed. They had travelled quite a distance and, had they not known their place so well, it would have been impossible for them to pick it out at such a distance.

Alyana looked tired. She was no longer young. Fifty summers, maybe more. She had been mother to other children who had died before Emlik and his sisters had been born. As they rested, she looked back towards the ocean. Emlik noticed how the sun danced on her silver hair. She must have been quite beautiful, he thought, as beautiful, perhaps as were her daughters.

"Here, Mother, I will take your load a while," Emlik proffered, as he raised her pack in one hand and helped her to her feet with the other. She smiled at him and gently cupped his cheek in her hand.

"Your father will never be dead as long as you are with us," she said. They smiled gently at each other.

The others had already got to their feet and Emlik again led the way, knowing, from his journey of the day before, that they were nearer now to the new place than to the old. They disappeared around the back of the grey and craggy mountain and headed for their new home.

The sun was reddening the sky by the time they neared their destination. A bronze tint coated the massive limestone hill behind them. Emlik stopped where the rock on which they walked came to an end, making a cliff, below which there was a green and fertile pasture.

"Listen," he said.

They were silent, not knowing what they were listening for. Frayika was the first to hear it.

"Water! Running water!" she shouted, dancing and turning towards Raithnika and Alyana, delighted that she had heard it first.

"Are we here, Emlik? Have we arrived?" Raithnika asked, coming forward to the edge of the rock.

"Yes, we have arrived. This is our new home," he said.

All four stood out on the cliff edge and looked down on the greenness spread before them. They inhaled its beauty. They had found a home at last.

3

Knapper, Death threatens, New Friends

It was early Spring when Emlik and his family had first come to their new home, nestled between the high places. Much time was spent clearing many of the nearby bushes and setting up their working area. By the time that Summer came the womenfolk had open huts, made of hides and wattles, where they could treat and hang the skins and in which they stored the stoneware bowls and querns which they had laboured hard to make.

Emlik too had been busy. Shortly after coming there, he had planted seeds of corn which they had brought with them from their homeland. He hoped that they would flourish, and indeed, by midsummer, it was obvious from the fresh young shoots that stood like lines of soldiers in a green patch by the river, that the harvest would be generous.

They had also managed to capture some wild animals and enclosed them in a compound, gradually widening its size and allowing them space in which to move. Eventually, when they were tamed, they removed the fencing, letting them roam freely about the settlement. There were two of the animals of the type which had chased and almost killed Emlik and which now they called 'the spotted ones'. They also had two goats, captured on the mountain by Emlik. One of these gave them a daily yield of milk which, they believed, gave strength and nourishment to their bones. It was because of this food, Alyana said, that their bones and teeth were white.

And then there was Knapper! Knapper was a wild dog which Frayika had found injured where the foot of the mountain had met the better ground. He was wolf. They had nursed him back to health and had tamed him so that, when he was well again, he stayed with them and became Emlik's companion in the hunt and a friend to all the others. The tip of his nose resembled a button and so, Frayika, for whom he always showed a particular fondness, had named him Knapper. Knapper, in their Nordic language, meant 'button'.

Even fortune had favoured them. Once, when Raithnika was rinsing skins in the stream, her bracelet of coloured beads dropped into the water and was swept with the current. It was a treasured possession because her father had made it for her when she was a mere seven summers. Emlik followed the stream in search of it and found it in a place where silt had lodged, just before their stream joined up with another. Somehow, he felt he knew this other stream and, sure enough, he found that when he travelled its course, it took him to the dunes. It was the stream by which they had made their first camp. And so Emlik was able, some days later, to take a small raft to the dunes and then return with their bronze cauldron mounted on it.

So, after all their hardship — their battle with the sea, the loss of Relco, and Emlik's own near death — the family had not only survived, but they had prospered far better and far more quickly than ever they might have dreamed. There was nothing else that they could ask for, except perhaps wider company. They often wondered about the hunters whom Emlik had seen when he stumbled on the new place. Where had they come from? Were they near at hand now? Were they friendly? Alyana, in her wisdom of age, had cautioned against haste. Time, she said, would reveal all things.

One day, towards the end of Summer, when the crop down by the river was high and golden, Frayika and Knapper had walked south into the hills. She was amazed at what she saw. In every direction, for as far as the eye could see, there were huge, flat, grey slabs. A gigantic limestone floor spread before her. In narrow slits between the slabs lived flowers of rare and wonderful beauty. For a long time, she moved from slab to slab, bending low to smell the many flowers and admire their vibrant colours.

"Aren't they beautiful, Knapper?"

And Knapper had licked her face, which Frayika

knew meant 'Yes, they are just the most beautiful flowers a wolf like me has ever seen.'

Frayika was so enthralled at the beauty she had found around her that she had not noticed the passage of the sun low into the southern sky. Neither had she paid any attention to the fact that it was morning since she had eaten. But Nature has her ways. Knapper's belly rolled a long and twisted pang.

"Ah, are you getting hungry, Knapper?" she asked, lovingly holding Knapper's head against her cheek. And, in asking, she realised that she herself was quite hungry now and that if Knapper's belly rolled, then it was night-time. Suddenly it struck her that she had absolutely no idea where they were. Which way back to the settlement? From what direction had they come? She looked all around her. Everything was the same. Flat, grey rock stretching out for thousands of paces in all directions. No tree, no bush, no running water to help her figure out where she had come from. Her heart quickened with worry.

Knapper then ran on in the direction of the southern sun. Soon it would be in the west, and then darkness. Then what? When he had gone two hundred paces or so, he looked back at Frayika and barked. He continued his bark until Frayika made her way to him. She crouched beside him and rested her arm on his shoulder.

"What is it, Knapper? Why are you barking?"

Knapper stopped now and looked out in the direction of the sun. Frayika followed his gaze.

"What is it, Knapper? Do you see something?"

Again, the dog took off and went another hundred paces or so, stopped as before and began to bark. Frayika followed quickly, crouched and looked ahead. This time she could see smoke rising in the distance. They must be near their settlement!

"Good boy, Knapper," she said, hugging the dog in to her. She kissed his button nose and then wiped the cold wetness of the contact from her lips.

They made their way quickly across the limestone floor until they reached a track down below the level of the rock. She did not know this track, but then there was much about the settlement that she had yet to learn and besides, this day was the first time she had ever strayed so far from base. To the left, the track continued on for quite some distance before bending its way from sight. To the right, it disappeared almost immediately, hiding itself behind the mass of rock on which Knapper and Frayika stood.

Looking out across the track, Frayika could see smoke rising from the bushes and, at almost the same time, she caught the smell of roasting meat wafting on the breeze.

"Knapper, you clever dog!" she cried, stooping to let him lick her face.

They descended onto the track and crossed into the hazel bushes which, at this time of year, were thick with leaves. Knapper led and, as they progressed, the smell of the burning meat got stronger, making Frayika even more aware of her hunger.

In places, among the bushes, the undergrowth was trampled, showing signs that others had often travelled here. It must have been a path that Emlik used at times, when returning from a day's hunting in the mountains. The strengthening smell and a thinning of the bushes suggested that she was nearing camp. Knapper had gone ahead and was out of sight now.

Then, suddenly, two heavy-set and rugged men jumped out in front of Frayika; a third rushed from behind and placed his forearm tightly across her neck. Frayika was thrown into shock, stunned by the suddenness and speed of their movements. They seemed more animal than human to her. Her heart thumped, knees weakened and, though she opened her mouth to scream, no noise came out.

These men were rough. Unlike Emlik, who was tall and clean of face, they were stocky and bearded. Their hair was dark and the skins they wore were the coats of the wild boar. The two to the front held the points of their spears to Frayika's stomach, pressing them against her. She was afraid to breathe for fear that one of them might pierce her skin. The one behind was shouting at the others in a language that Frayika had never heard before. Her eyes moved rapidly from side to side. She feared what the one who held her may have been saying. One of the two before her removed his spear from her stomach, came forward and yanked the string of coloured stones from her neck. She screamed, a long sharp scream that scythed through the air and alarmed the men. The one who held the spear against her pierced her with the weapon and again Frayika screamed. Again he prodded with the spearhead, thinking maybe that this might shut her up. It had the opposite effect — she screamed a third time and the man behind, who still held on tightly, cupped his huge hand across her mouth.

All of a sudden, Knapper sprang forward from the bushes, sprawling himself in mid-air and hurtling all his weight against the one who had speared Frayika. Knapper knocked him to the ground and bit his flailing arms and legs. The second man danced threateningly around the dog, trying to spike him with the spear, but afraid at the same time that, if he missed, he might injure his comrade. Frayika, heartened by Knapper's effort, sank her teeth hard into the fleshy palm that gagged her. Her captor released her, clutching his hand, which now was bleeding badly. Knapper shifted his attention from the man on the ground and went at the legs of the one who had held Frayika. He snapped at his calves and the anguished man shouted angrily across at the one still holding the spear. The spear-bearer approached and again danced around cautiously. Then, seizing his chance and believing his aim was true, he released the weapon, missing Knapper completely and wounding his own kinsman in the leg. Then, fearing that Knapper might turn his attention onto him, the third man took flight.

The other two attackers were mesmerised and were so concerned with their own injuries that it gave

Knapper the chance to grip Frayika's wrist gently between his jaws and to lead her back through the hazel bushes to safety. Frayika was bleeding badly and, as soon as Knapper was fairly sure of their own safety, he stopped and drew her away from the track and into the middle of the copse. He located a spot beneath the bushes that was dry and warm. Then he crouched, drawing Frayika to her knees. Almost as if she knew it was safe to do so now, Frayika fainted, falling in the spot which Knapper had sought out. The dog dragged fern and twigs from the undergrowth and placed them over the girl, ensuring that, even if the marauders should come this way, they would be unlikely to see her.

There was a brightness in Knapper's eyes, the brightness of intelligence. Instinctively, he knew what he must do. He pricked his ears, looked keenly to both sides and then backed his way out from among the bushes. He headed for the clear track which earlier he had found at the edge of the limestone mass. Once there, he cocked his head and gave a long and searching howl.

"Owwwwwwwwwwwww!"

The crescent of the moon hung, like a sharpened sickle, high over Moneen Mountain.

"Ow, Ow, Ow-Ow-Owwww!" he heard in the distance.

"Ow Ow!" Knapper snapped in retort.

"Ow Ow Owwww!" came the answer again.

Knapper turned his head sharply to where the

track disappeared behind the limestone. That was the direction of the distant cry. He ran back into the bushes to where Frayika lay, checked that things were just as he had left them, then bounded out again onto the track and followed it beyond the bend that would take him to a place he had not seen before. Every now and then he'd howl his cry, "Ow, Ow", and each and every time the response came back: "Ow, Ow, Owwww!" All the time, he was getting nearer and he could tell now that the calls he heard were not of the wild. They were the cries of wolves who, just like himself, had been tamed. And tamed wolves meant humans. And humans meant help! But what if they were the same humans at whose hands they had already suffered? He must be careful. He would know quite quickly if they were to be trusted.

Knapper had ceased his howling now. He had got his bearings and knew exactly the location from which he had received the responses. He moved off the track and in amongst the bushes. Lying on his belly, he made his way forward, working his legs both front and back to project himself along the ground. There was water and a high earthen bank ahead. He jumped the water and, carefully, inched his way up the bank, reclining his ears so as to lessen his chances of being seen. As his eyes cleared the top of the bank, the yellow warmth of firelight danced in his pupils. He pricked his ears. Humans! Fifteen or twenty of them, he thought. Men, women and some young ones too. They sat around a huge fire, laughing and talking.

They were enclosed by a perfect earthen circle which was lined with trees. The upper branches reached in towards the centre so that they touched one another, forming a perfect shelter from the elements. Knapper's instinct told him that there was a warmth and a friendliness about this place.

He pulled himself up and stood on top of the bank and, as he did, the wolf-dogs he had earlier heard now came running towards him, wagging their tails, barking and acting playfully. There were six of them. Two of the humans left the fire and came towards Knapper. They had clean chins and wore skins of white wool, and Knapper knew immediately that they were not kinsmen of those who had attacked Frayika in the bushes. He allowed the men to stroke his coat and he nuzzled up to them, winning their affection. When he sensed there was a mutual trust, he moved away from them and again began to howl. He then moved back, and then away and howled again. He made to dart off even further, but stopped again to howl and to look at these men. These were men who knew the ways of the wolf. Had they not tamed such animals themselves! He wanted them to follow. They ran back towards the campfire and each grabbed a spear, a stone axe and a lighted torch, and came back again towards Knapper. The faithful dog disappeared down the bank, leaped the water and led them out onto the track. Darkness had fallen, enshrouding the stony greyness for another night.

Within minutes, they were at the point where

Frayika lay. Knapper gently pawed the covering of fern and twigs from her body and then stood back, allowing the men to tend to her. The taller of the two handed his torch to his comrade and then picked Frayika up in his arms. He nodded to the other man to lead them from the bushes.

Soon they were back at the encampment. The women there attended to Frayika's wound, while the men readied an area in which she could sleep. They piled straw in abundance into a huge hollowed-out tree trunk which they had felled when clearing the middle of their settlement, and which, up to now, had provided an opportunity for play to the children of their camp.

Once Frayika had been treated, she was laid in the tree trunk, which now had been drawn up near to the fire. The men and women sat discussing what they should do. Who was she? Where had she come from? Every now and then one of the women fingered Frayika's golden hair, marvelling at the way it captured the light of the fire. They had never seen such colouring of hair or of skin before. Their hair was brown and their skin was darker than Frayika's, with a red tint in the face.

Knapper lay alongside the tree trunk. His chin rested on his two outstretched paws and his eyes moved dreamily from one person to another, arching his brows as he listened to the conversation. He knew he had fallen into good company. Suddenly his ears stood upright and his eyes danced to attention; he lifted his head and then raised himself fully from his lying position. Yet again, he howled another of his long howls and darted to the wooden bridge that formed an entrance to the encampment. He was followed by the dogs of the settlement. The men around the camp-fire jumped up and grabbed their weapons. There were six of them, including the two who had saved Frayika. They too followed Knapper to the exit. Knapper howled again and was followed by a chorus from the other dogs.

The men could hear the rustle of foliage in the distance. Three of them crossed the settlement again in a hurry and exited at the back, taking their dogs with them and intending to come around behind the marauders. To the front, the other three held onto Knapper, waiting. Then, about one hundred yards up the track, in the direction of the marauders' settle-ment, the bright burning of a torch appeared. The three at the entrance stood back behind the two huge oaks that formed a portal to the settlement. Suddenly Knapper ran out and made directly for the torchlight. Though it was earlier than they might have wished, the men at the entrance knew that they must attack. They rushed forward after Knapper, shouting cries of battle and readying for the fray. From the rear, the others and their dogs came in similar fashion. Next thing the torch was lowered and, as the light fell upon Knapper, it revealed him jumping up and licking the face of the oncoming stranger. It was Emlik. He had come searching for his sister.

"Knapper, Knapper, what a good dog! What a good dog!" said Emlik.

Emlik was just about to brace himself again for the onslaught when the others realised that the dog had found his master. They lowered their weapons and their leader came forward to Emlik and stood before him. They looked firmly at each other and Knapper toed and froed, creating shadows in the torchlight and rubbed his head against the thighs of the two men. The stranger reached his arm towards Emlik, and Emlik, realising that this was a gesture of welcome, reached out his own arm towards the stranger. They clasped each other firmly, each closing his hand on the forearm of the other, just above the wrist.

"Fáilte," the leader said.

Emlik looked at him. This was not his language, but he sensed from the warmth of their handshake and the smile which accompanied the utterance that he was being made welcome. Emlik could not have known then, nor indeed could have Cneasán, leader of this clan, that theirs was to be a friendship that would last a lifetime.

A short time later, back in the camp, Emlik knelt over his sister. She had regained consciousness and was smiling up at him. One of the women came, wiped Frayika's forehead with a cool cloth and gently pinched her cheek in encouragement. Emlik, though shocked at first, could see now that his sister was safe and was fortunate to have fallen into good hands.

Cneasán beckoned to Emlik to sit beside him at the

fire. He took a twig and, in the loose clay that surrounded the fire, he indicated the location of their settlement and then the settlement of those responsible for the attack on Frayika. He offered the twig to Emlik so that he too could demonstrate where his own settlement was in relation to these two.

Not having a common language, they gestured to each other for a long time. Emlik learned of Cneasán's clan, that they were twenty-eight in number, that they had once occupied the *Cathair Mhór* — Cahermore — a stone fort, now the settlement of the marauders, or the Barbey as they were known. But Cneasán and his people had been violently ousted from it some years earlier; it was then that they had come to settle in their new place, which they called Ballyallaban — 'the settlement of the white cliff', so-called because of the whiteness of the limestone cliff beyond.

Emlik too, through gestures, shared all knowledge of his own people, telling of their coming, of his father's death and of Darkon's disappearance. He learned that Cneasán and his people knew the area of Emlik's settlement as Loch Reasc, 'the lake of the marshy place'. Though to Emlik's knowledge, there was no lake there, he thought that perhaps there was one in the vicinity which he had not yet discovered.

Such was the warmth of the welcome and so engaging their efforts at conversation that Emlik did not feel the time slip by. Suddenly, he thought of Alyana and Raithnika. They were back at their settlement, anxious about Frayika's absence, awaiting news of her. By now, they probably thought that whatever fate had befallen her had also befallen Emlik.

Emlik stood and approached Frayika. She was sleeping again. It was agreed that it was best not to move her; that she was welcome in Ballyallaban for however long was necessary. Emlik knelt by his sister and kissed her on the forehead. Knapper, who all this time lay beside her, rumbled a sound of contentment in his throat. Emlik stood now and reached his hand to Cneasán. They clasped arms as before, then embraced and heartily patted each other on the back.

"Thank you, friend Cneasán," Emlik said.

"And long may we be friends," replied Cneasán.

Though they could not understand each other's utterance, they looked into each other's eyes and knew that, for all that was bad that happened on this day, their meeting could yield nothing but that which was good.

"Come on, Knapper. Come on, boy," said Emlik.

He crossed the wooden bridge, and Knapper, the brave and faithful dog, followed, stopping as he crossed the moat to look back at Cneasán and his people. He lifted his head high and howled a final howl that pierced the silence of the night, and then ran after his master.

4

Friendship and Marriage,
The Story of Loch Reasc, Tragedy

Winter followed Summer, and then Winter and then Summer yet again. And so it went, until many summers had passed since that night when Frayika had been saved by Knapper. The family in Loch Reasc had grown and further clearing of the bushes had happened so as to accommodate their increasing number. Ballyallaban and Loch Reasc were as one, all but for the distance that separated them physically from each other.

Since their first meeting, Cneasán and Emlik grew in friendship. Often they and their kinsfolk visited each other's camps, worked and hunted together, shared their sorrows and their joys. As his senior and being of this limestone land which, as Emlik had long since learned, was called Burren, Cneasán had much to teach his younger friend. The ways of the Celt were different to what Emlik and his people knew, and there was much to learn.

Now a man of thirty-five summers, Emlik had married Orla, sister of Cneasán. They had three children: Relco, named after his grandfather, whom he had never known, was tall and fair and had the blue eyes of his father. His sisters, Deirbhile and Sobharthan, were darker, more like their mother. Already Relco, who was now fourteen summers, had been trained in the arts of the hunt and of the fight. So too were Deirbhile and Sobharthan, a decision which both Orla and her husband had agreed upon.

Raithnika too had taken a husband, Fearchú, a kinsman of Cneasán, and one renowned for his great bravery. Motherhood suited her, and her children, Saoirse, a girl, and Fionnán, a boy, bore the perfect mix of their parents' traits. They had founded their own settlement, Lios an Rú, at the foot of Cappanawalla, the great limestone hill not far to the west of Cneasán's camp. Soon after, they were joined by other kinsfolk from the Ballyallaban site.

As for Alyana and Frayika, they were still in Loch Reasc. It seemed however that, for different reasons, their lives too would change. Frayika, who had grown to be a very beautiful woman, even more beautiful than her sister, was being wooed by Fiachra, a herdsman from a settlement to the far south. It was felt that, in time, she would leave Loch Reasc to settle with his people.

Alyana was ageing. For a time, the coming of grandchildren had rekindled her enthusiasm but, in the past year, her mind was rambling. In the nighttime she was often heard to cry out her husband's name, Relco. She had taken to walking to the nearby stream while still sleeping. One day Emlik talked to her about this.

"The Animal is calling me to be with Relco," she said.

"Look, Mother, look around you," Emlik replied in frustration. "There is no animal except those which are our own."

"He is calling me. I hear him in my sleep. He is standing out on Moneen Mountain, calling to me, telling me that Relco is waiting for me to join him."

"No, Mother, it is your imagination. Your mind is playing with you."

Alyana was persistent and Emlik knew better than to continue debating with her. Time would take its toll when it was ready. By now, of course, the Celtic language of Cneasán and his people had become their common speech. Emlik often thought back to the first night he had heard it spoken — the night they met their neighbours — and how, through their gestures, he and Cneasán made sense of each other's thoughts. Until then, it had never dawned on him that there were other ways to communicate one's thoughts. He had only ever heard his own language and had no reason to think that there could possibly be any other. Nowadays, he so rarely spoke his own Nordic tongue that he could not be sure of his ability to still use it.

Earlier this particular year, *Lughnasa*, the feast of the great god Lugh, had been celebrated at Loch Reasc. They had come from Ballyallaban and from Lios an Rú to make their offerings to the deity. The crops this summer had been good. Emlik had planted many times the amount of corn that he had planted the first summer that they had come there. The wooden huts within the settlement were filled with the harvest. At Ballyallaban and Lios an Rú it was the same. There was much for which to be thankful.

And so all the work was done, and now the Winter feast of *Samhain* was fast approaching — the time when Man and Beast surrendered the next half-year to the hands of the gods. No sowing and very little hunting would be done. Winter would be long and dark, and there would be little travel between the settlements. Their lives would be committed to the Daghda, the Good God, who was all-seeing and all-powerful. They would gather at Ballyallaban on *Oíche Shamhna* — the Eve of Samhain — to bid farewell awhile to some of Nature's wonders and to one another.

Samhain is a time of cold and dark whispers. It is the time when the Spiritworld takes back all that it has loaned to Man and Nature. Over the years they had heard from Cneasán and the others tales of goblins and of great winds, of happenings with clouds and fire, and of people taken to satisfy the Daghda. And so, it was with great respect for the Otherworld that the families came to Ballyallaban.

"You are welcome, my friends," Cneasán said heartily, as he embraced his neighbours, now kinsfolk from Loch Reasc. All but Alyana had come. She was too feeble now. When they left, she was sleeping, and Knapper, now old himself, but every bit as faithful as when he was young, stayed to watch over the old woman.

The others from Lios an Rú had arrived before them and were seated round the fire. It had been some time since they had seen their people from Loch Reasc. The harvest had been good and plentiful and this had kept the families busy, limiting their opportunities to visit one another.

"What of Alyana?" Fearchú asked.

"She is not strong," said Orla. "The journey here would be too much for her."

"Very soon she will make the greatest journey of them all," Sobharthan interjected. All looked at her. It was known amongst the families that Sobharthan, though only twelve summers, had been given the gift of vision. Her dark eyes looked deep beyond this world and saw that which was lighted on the other side.

There was a silence. Still they looked at the young girl. Though they knew Alyana was unlikely to survive the winter, there was an uneasiness about what the child had said. Just as the silence neared discomfort, Cneasán spoke.

"Come, come, my friends. We have come to celebrate and to wish one another well. Let us be joyous and light-hearted. There are many dark nights ahead of us before Mighty Imbolc, God of Spring, comes to fill the udders of our ewes again."

"You are right, Cneasán," Raithnika said.

"Aye," said Frayika. "Let us celebrate all that is

good." And she raised her goblet, filled with the steaming redness of wine made from the berry of the white bush that flourished by their settlement.

"To all that is good!" Cneasán said, now standing and raising his own goblet.

"To all that is good!" said the others in unison.

As they drank, Emlik looked out across the rim of his goblet and caught the eye of his younger daughter. She smiled. Sobharthan was a child of great love. She had been given the gift of vision but, at times, when vision told of things unpleasant, she felt her gift a great burden upon her. It was a comfort to her that her father understood.

Of the many years and feasts celebrated in Ballyallaban no one could remember so great and splendid a fire as that which burned this night of Samhain. The trees around the camp danced in its light and overhead, the stars of the night peered through what was now a thinning umbrella of foliage. Cneasán and his wife Mánla had made great preparation for their guests. Above the fire, two animals were roasting — one a sheep, specially selected from Cneasán's flock; the other a boar, fattened in the wilderness, never knowing that he would be a centre-piece on the Feast of Samhain.

As the adults sat around the fire, drinking and conversing, the younger children played games of skill behind them. One group had mounted the skin of a squirrel on a tree trunk and, in turns, they threw a spear at it to see which of them had the keenest eye.

Others played 'Release the Goat', a game of speed which Fearchú had taught them. And others, still, were engrossed in stringing nuts, which had fallen from the trees. There was a sense of excitement in the camp; the gaiety of kinsfolk being together, enjoying one another's company.

Cneasán walked out from the adults and clapped his hands: "Come on now, children. It is time to eat." The meats had been carved and laid out on huge wooden platters. The children gathered in and it wasn't long until, between themselves and the adults, all was eaten. They returned then to their play and the adults to their conversation.

"My friends," Cneasán said, standing and interrupting the conversation, "there is something I wish to say." They were silent and all looked at this elder of their number. "It is eighteen summers since I first met my great friend, Emlik. Since then, many moons have filled the Burren sky. Our bond of friendship strengthened and then became a bond of kinship. Our numbers mingled and grew, so that, after our summers of friendship, we are three groups, all closely tied to one another."

The assembly looked on, nodding to each other, showing approval of all that Cneasán said. "Because it is the Feast of Samhain, the time when we say farewell to the old and look forward, in expectation, to the new, I wish to seal that bond of friendship with these gifts."

Turning then to Mánla, who stood beside him as he

spoke, he took two items from her. "This," he said, holding up a beautifully adorned collar of pure gold, "is the golden collar of Gleninsheen, a thing of great age, handed down to me by my forefathers."

Emlik had come forward and Cneasán placed the bright gold collar around his neck.

"And this," said Cneasán, holding aloft a spear with a head of darkened metal, "is of the new; soon it will replace our spearheads of stone and bronze." He handed Emlik this new spear. Emlik looked at the etchings on the spearhead. They were made in random fashion and did not hold the beauty or the craftsmanship born on the collar of gold. But the metal was hard, harder than anything he had ever felt before.

The two men embraced and the drone of talk amongst the others indicated their satisfaction that the bond between the families was stronger now than ever. The conversation fell into song and storytelling. Tales not told and songs not sung since at least the Samhain before were rendered by the company. Then a lull came in the revelry. It was a time of that kind which makes one speak a thought that has lingered long in the back of the mind.

"Tell us of Loch Reasc, Cneasán." It was Emlik who spoke.

"What?" asked Cneasán, somewhat surprised. "What about Loch Reasc?"

"Many summers ago," said Emlik, "when first we met, you spoke of a lake at Loch Reasc; but I have not yet seen a lake to any side of it."

Cneasán looked steadily at his friend. It was obvious from the concern in his eyes that he was pondering whether or not he should speak. Eventually he did. "There is a story," he said slowly, almost hesitantly, and then he paused, "but perhaps tonight is not the time to tell such things."

The listeners around the fire, whose expectations had been raised by Cneasán's utterance, muttered their disgruntlement at the suggestion that this story would not be told, for not only had their interest been aroused, but it was also acknowledged among the families that Cneasán was a storyteller of great skill.

"Surely, Cneasán," said Fearchú, "if ever a time is right to tell a story, it is this night." The assembly murmured agreement with Fearchú's words. Cneasán looked to Emlik again, a look tinged still with apprehension.

"All right, all right," he said, lowering himself onto his hunkers.

The circled gathering drew a little closer to the fire. They smiled at one another, happy that their persistence had succeeded in persuading Cneasán to tell the story of Loch Reasc.

"It was my father who told me this tale," he began. "He had heard it from his own father, and he in turn from his father before him. Many summers ago, when first our people came to the land of the Burren, we settled, as you know, just south of here and built our fort, the Cathair Mhór, which now is occupied by the Barbey."

All in the gathering knew this much, for each and every one of them had learned of the Barbey, of their ferociousness and of the necessity to avoid them at all times.

"Well, what none of you will have heard before and what I am about to tell you is that we, and the others who had settled in all directions, would, if they had had their choice, have settled on the land that we know as Loch Reasc."

"Where Emlik and his people are!" exclaimed Mánla.

"Exactly," said Cneasán. "It was, and is again, the very best land at the foot of the Burren. But for all that, it remained unoccupied by man for many many summers.

"Well, why didn't our family occupy it?" asked one of the younger men.

"Patience, son," said Cneasán, and as he said it, he could see the light of understanding in the eyes of Emlik's daughter, Sobharthan, the Seer. He thought that he had, perhaps, gone too far already and that this story would have been better left untold. But now he knew that, were he to stop, he would not only bring the anger of the others on him, but also leave them in doubt, creating imaginings in their minds, even worse than anything he might tell them. He picked up a twig that lay on the ground beside him; it was brittle with age. Then, standing, he walked away from the fire, stood with his back to his kinsmen and thought a little. He snapped the twig between his fingers, turned and eased himself onto his hunkers once again. He looked towards Sobharthan, but she had lowered her head and was looking at the ground before her. He began again.

"Very many summers ago, when the people of my people's people came to the land of the Burren, there was before us, in the area of Loch Reasc, another clan who fished the waters and tilled the fields. They were, I have been told, a gentle and an understanding people. They were friends of Nature, of all they found around them."

Cneasán's family looked on intently as their leader spoke. No one dared to interrupt him, for already they had seen that the decision to relate this story had been made with considerable difficulty. "For some reason, which I have not been told, one of their young men incurred the wrath of a wicked *cailleach*, a hag, far to the south of these lands. As a punishment she, it is said, cursed the young man and all his people and all their lands. *Mallacht na nGabhar* — The Curse of the Goats — was the curse that she had put on them."

The Curse of the Goats was not a curse of which any of Cneasán's listeners had ever heard before. They looked at one another, bewitched by the artistry of Cneasán's telling of this tale. They could feel that little strain of fear that makes one want to hear more, running through the blood inside their veins.

"Time passed and little was thought or spoken of the curse this hag had put upon the people of Loch

Reasc. Then one night, some summers later, as the people of Loch Reasc gathered on the Eve of Samhain, just as we have gathered here tonight, night closed in dark and hard around their settlement, and with it came —"

"The Goat!" Sobharthan interjected, with a certainty that made the speaker stop. Cneasán looked at Sobharthan, as indeed they all did. He knew she could read his thoughts before he spoke them and this made him feel uncomfortable in himself. His only consolation was that Sobharthan, as each and every one of them knew, was a seer filled with goodness. Cneasán reached across to her and squeezed her hand.

"And with it came the Goat," he continued. "A herd of goats, fleet of foot from their climbing of the Burren stone, and sharp of horn. As the humans slept, they surged with a vengeance into the camp, over-turning huts and pots, knocking children from their beds and traipsing through the fire, scattering lighted embers onto the crops that had been carefully stored in the winter keep. When this was done, the goats assembled in the middle of the camp and looked towards the limestone cliff that, to this very day, sits beyond the camp. There, a huge black ram stood. The reflection of the scattered embers filled his eyes. He looked down on the other goats and then, lifting his head high towards the stars of the night, he bleated a long, loud call that was a message to the others. Immediately the goats ran riot within the camp.

Women grabbed their children and men their spears, in an effort to quell the rampage. Within minutes, all but the goats remained. The bodies of the occupants, each and every one of them — man, woman, child — lay dead, gored by the horns of the goats. The grass within the settlement was a sea of red.

"On the hill, the black ram again lifted his head up towards the sky and again he bleated a loud bleat, that ranged far out into the night. Suddenly the earth trembled and a long squelching sound came from where the devastation lay and, as the black ram looked on, the settlement before him filled with water, engulfing every one and every thing that lay within the camp. The ram stood watching as the lake formed before his eyes. Once formed, he lifted his head for the third time, bleated, and then looked down to watch the lake recede beneath the earth. Everything was as it had been, except that now there were no signs of humans or of their settlement, or indeed, of the goats who had visited such terrible destruction on the camp. It was as beautiful and as green and as fertile a spot as ever it had been. And that, my people, is the story of Loch Reasc."

There was a silence around the campfire. People looked at each other, enthralled both at Cneasán's artistry in his telling of this tale and at the fact that it was one which they never before had heard.

"But what of the black ram? What happened to him?" asked Fearchú.

"It is said that he climbed high into the mountain

and that his spirit still watches over Loch Reasc," replied Cneasán.

"And the lake, Cneasán?" said Emlik. "Where is the lake now?"

"Who knows, my friend! Who knows! It is only a story; one which was created by our fathers before us, to pass away the long, dark wintry nights."

Again there was a silence. A gentle breeze rose somewhere in the distant south and made its way to the settlement at Ballyallaban, making a rustling sound in the thin cover of leaves overhead. Those around the fire came closer to its heat and pulled their furs and skins tighter around them.

The breeze grew stronger; the kinsfolk looked above their heads and, through the openings in the foliage, they could see a sweeping cloud eat the stars of night. Then, as if to chase away this southern breeze, a sudden gust came down off Moneen Mountain, meeting it and causing the air to swirl around Ballyallaban.

The gust strengthened now; it was as if the breezes fought against each other for supremacy. Leaves overhead, already sparse, were swept from the trees now and a definite chill made its way inside the settlement. The wooden embers of the fire reddened where the wind had blown their dusty coats from them. Suddenly, a roll, as if of thunder, rumbled through the air and made its way towards Ballyallaban. Once overhead, it seemed to release itself with a burst, sending all the leaves swirling within the encampment. The wind blew much harder now and the rain lashed in anger. The children, who had already made their way into the huts, were followed by the adults.

The rain poured, the wind howled and the leaves swirled with a vengeance for many heartbeats, and then there was quiet. The silence was eerie, as eerie as Cneasán's telling of the tale of Loch Reasc. Suddenly Sobharthan looked at Emlik, then Emlik at Cneasán and then Cneasán back to Sobharthan.

"Alyana!" said Sobharthan.

All three moved now with great speed, followed by Fearchú and Relco. As they neared the camp at Loch Reasc, Emlik called, "Knapper, Knapper!"

There was no reply. Instinctively he knew that things were not right. They rushed into the camp and made immediately for Alyana's hut. It was empty.

"Knapper, here boy! Knapper!"

This time it was Cneasán who called the dog. Again, no answer.

"The river!" said Emlik, in startled realisation. The men looked wide-eyed at one another, sensing that Emlik's fear might be well-founded. Only Sobharthan knew for certain that Emlik was correct.

At the bottom of the riverbank, Knapper's body lay across Alyana's. His effort to protect her had been in vain. Emlik fell to his knees by their side and looked in horror at where they had been gored. The same marks that had taken Relco to his death. Emlik stood and looked out at the sky, now clear again over Moneen Mountain.

"The Animal!" said Sobharthan, staring out in the same direction. The others turned to look at her.

5

*Burial, More about the Barbey,
Further Tragedy, Sobharthan's Visions,
Attack on Deirbhile*

They had come to the place of the Great Standing
Stones, high up in the Burren and beyond the yellow
cliff which they called Aillwee. Raithnika held the
earthen pot into which, some days earlier, they had
gathered Alyana's ashes from the pyre. Frayika, to her
left, held those of Knapper. It was not the custom to
treat animals with the same importance as the human,
but Knapper had been brother, father, guardian and
defender of this family. They differed from him only
in that they had two legs and so could not run as fast
as him.

"Come forward," said Emlik to his sisters. He held
a bronze pot, larger than either of the earthen ones
which his sisters carried. Emlik took the pot from
Raithnika and emptied its contents into the bronze
one. And then Frayika's. Then he swirled the ashes in
the metal container, mixing animal with human and
human with animal. He now moved to the west end
of the Standing Stones and raised the metal pot
against the setting sun. He chanted some words in the

language of his homeland and then lowered the pot again. He turned to face his family and, one by one, Raithnika, Frayika, Cneasán and Fearchú came forward, took a handful of dust from the pot and cast it in turn to the north, the south, the east and the west. When this was done, Emlik placed the golden collar which Cneasán had given to him on the Eve of Samhain into the bronze container.

Raithnika, elder of the daughters, took the pot with the golden collar and the remaining ashes, entered the chamber of the Standing Stones and placed it carefully against the backing slab. Then Mánla entered, bearing with her some golden torcs and pins, and placed them inside the pot. And finally Frayika entered the chamber and placed a quern, now old and shiny, against the pot. It was one which Alyana had used for many years when grinding corn.

Cneasán came forward to his friend, Emlik. "It is done and done well," he said. "Alyana would be pleased."

"Her spirit is with Relco now," said Emlik. "It is all she wanted since he went from us."

"Let us leave the mountain now, or shortly we will share it with the night. Come," said Cneasán.

They made their way down the mountain, coming in time to a ridge, below which lay a track. Thor, the young dog whom they hoped would, in time, be as great a servant to them as was Knapper, stood on the ledge and whined. Frayika came to him, stooped and hugged him. Her attachment to this dog was a continuation of the love she felt for Knapper.

"Don't be afraid, Thor. You won't have to jump." As she spoke, she looked out across the track and saw a mass of hazel bushes, now leafless; suddenly, a sense of having been in this place before came rushing back to her. She was just about to scream when she felt a hand on her shoulder. She turned. It was her brother's child, Sobharthan. She placed the back of her hand against Frayika's cheek.

"It is all right, Frayika. You will not be harmed." They both looked beyond the track and, visible through the bare trees, was the stone of Cahermore.

"It is the place of the Barbey," said Cneasán. "Let us go quietly and quickly on our way."

They moved with speed and as they disappeared down the track and behind the limestone hill, the bleat of a poc goat in the distance pierced the silence of the night. They were unaware that all this time they had been watched.

Emlik and his family stopped a while at Ballyallaban before continuing home that night. While there, many things were discussed, not least of all the Barbey.

"Our paths and theirs have not crossed since the day of Frayika's injuries many summers ago," said Emlik.

"That is as is best," said Cneasán. "They understand no law except their own, and even that, at times, is pushed aside."

"Is there any trouble being so near to them?" asked

Raithnika. "None since the time they ran us from our home at Cahermore," Mánla answered. "But one can never be too sure with them. If it is difficult for them to be nice to one another, it would be a great mistake for us to think that we were safe from their wild ways."

Fearchú spoke: "I have heard that recently they have appointed a new leader."

"Yes. Dubhán is his name," proffered Fiachra.

"Really!" exclaimed Frayika, surprised at Fiachra's knowledge and that he had not mentioned this before. "How do they elect him? Is he the son of the one who goes before him?"

"He is not elected, Frayika," said Fearchú, "and being the son of anyone is not important in the ways of the Barbey." He paused and looked hard in the direction of Cahermore. A steeliness came over his face: "They follow the ways of the great red elk of the wilderness — they fight for leadership!"

The others looked at one another, surprised that this should be so. Cneasán, however, knew the truth of what Fearchú had just revealed.

"To the death!" added Fearchú, bringing even greater silence and surprise to his listeners.

"What Fearchú says is true," said Cneasán, "but once we tend to our own business and they to theirs, we have no reason to fear the Barbey. Their hunting is to the south and all their crops are grown in the green valley beyond Aillwee Mountain."

"But surely —"

"I said we have no need to fear them, Relco," interrupted Cneasán. He looked at Emlik's son and then explained. "Their business is in Moneen Valley, where the land is fertile and it yields even more than their number would ever require."

Cneasán looked around him. He could see a nervousness in the faces of his friends and family. This was the first occasion in a long time that he could remember any lengthy discussion of the Barbey. He was just a boy when Cahermore had been ransacked by them and his people were driven out, many of them killed. He had a very clear memory of the ferocity of their attack. His own brother, Ultan, had died on a Barbey spear at that time and there was much bitterness between the settlements ever after.

Cneasán, however, was leader now at Ballyallaban and, above all else, his duty was to ensure the safety of his people. There was no sense in making them nervous about something that had happened so many summers back, or about anything that might or might not happen in the summers that were to come.

"We will leave it at that," he said.

His gaze met the deep and knowing eyes of Sobharthan. She smiled. Her smile was gentle and good. But even so, for reasons of a different sort, Cneasán felt nervous for his people.

Springtime came. The God of Gentleness, Imbolc, smiled blessings on the settlement at Loch Reasc. The ewes, numerous at this time of year, were filled with milk; the land, which the settlers had broadened over time, was tilled and ready for seed. Emlik led the young men out on to Moneen Mountain every day to hunt wild goat and boar. Having been confined to the settlements for the winter months, there was now a freshness and enthusiasm in their efforts. At the foot of Moneen Mountain, on the eastern side, was Moneen Valley — the fertile place where the Barbey grew their crops. Always Emlik cautioned the young men of the settlement not to encroach on these lands.

But often young men neither have nor heed the wisdom of the old. And so, one day, Fearghal, son of Orla's sister, Aoife, went to the eastern foot of Moneen Mountain while the others hunted rodents on the upper slopes. Fearghal had the curiosity of youth, but with it too, the foolishness to ignore the wisdom of his elders. Those on the mountain had not noticed that he was no longer with them. He made his way along the edge of the tilled valley until he came to a stream. This stream was the life-water to the valley; the Barbey named it Luirc and it was sacred to their people. Fearghal knelt and scooped a handful of the fresh-water to his mouth. It was refreshing and tasted good after the morning's work. He leaned forward to scoop a second handful, but this time, even though the water ran with force, he saw the reflection of a black goat's head in it. He jumped up with shock, ran across the stream and, as he reached the top of the bank on the other side, he stepped onto a solitary slab of limestone. Suddenly a huge wooden board, with nine metal spikes mounted on it, shot upright from the ground and ran him through.

There was but one single roar of pain. The others on the mountain turned to look. For some moments there was silence, but then their eyes adjusted and made sense of what they saw.

"No! No! It's Fearghal! It's Fearghal!" came the demented cry of Suibhne, Fearghal's father, who had been hunting on the mountain with the others. He bounded forward and was making his way down the mountain in the direction of his son.

"No, Suibhne, come back!" shouted Emlik in alarm. Suibhne ignored him and kept on going in the direction of his son. Emlik looked to his own son and quickly issued his instruction. "Stop him, Relco. Stop him before he meets the same fate."

Relco, though scarcely fifteen summers, was a man already. He had the skill and the speed that had been Emlik's when he was that age. He moved quickly now after Suibhne, bounding down the craggy slope, gaining on the older man all the time. Just as Suibhne reached the better ground, he was swooped upon by Relco. Despite his youth, the younger man had little difficulty in pinning Suibhne to the ground and holding him until the others had arrived.

Emlik stood over them now and spoke with authority. "There is nothing you can do now. He is dead, Suibhne. There is no sense in endangering your-self also. We can return when it is night-time and bring the body back to Loch Reasc. That way, nothing will be known of our presence here."

Suibhne looked up at Emlik and, despite his anguish and his grief, he knew that there was sense in what he said.

But Fearghal's body was not retrieved. When they came back that night, there was no sign of Fearghal or of the spiked board on which he had been impaled. The three of them, Emlik, Relco and Suibhne, returned to camp, not knowing if or when they would ever learn what had become of Fearghal. It was a time of great sorrow in the settlement of Loch Reasc.

More and more, these times, Emlik sought the counsel of his daughter, Sobharthan. She was nearing thirteen summers now and her power of vision was growing with her. She had noticed, however, that many of her visions were of troubles and of darkness and that, increasingly, fewer were joyful. Often, though she could see what lay ahead, she could not yet fully interpret the visions.

"What should we do about Fearghal's body?" her father asked one day, as they walked together along the perimeter of the settlement. Sobharthan answered him quite firmly: "Nothing."

"Nothing?"

"If you go in search of Fearghal's body, there will be great slaughter. I have seen this in a vision. If you leave things rest a while, then, in time, it will be returned."

Sobharthan, though a little older now, was still quite bothered by many of the visions that she had. Often she preferred to emphasise those which she believed foretold good. She stopped her father and pointed to a patch of ground before him. "Here, Father," she said enthusiastically, "will grow a plant that will spread all around our settlement. I will call it *Raithneach*, a fern, named after Raithnika."

"How do you —?"

"And here," she said, interrupting Emlik and running out a little further from the settlement, "will be a beautiful purple heather, as beautiful as Frayika. It will be named *Fraoch*, specially in her honour."

"*Raithneach* and *Fraoch*, huh!" said Emlik, pensively. "I'm sure Raithnika and Frayika will indeed be honoured to be counted among the flowers of the fields." He smiled at her. He knew her need not to be pressed too much about the visions. But the events surrounding the deaths of Alyana and of Knapper and now, more recently, of Fearghal too, alarmed him and put a pressure of a different kind on him.

"Sobharthan, *a stór*," he said, putting his arm across her shoulder and drawing her towards him, "you know that your mother and I love you very much, just as we love Deirbhile and Relco. They were lucky that they were not the ones given the power of vision. We know that, while it is a blessing, it is a curse also, because you are forced to carry the burden of what the visions may reveal to you."

Up to now Sobharthan had looked on and carefully listened to her father as he spoke. She had known from times before this that her father was sensitive to the difficulty of her situation.

"But this, Sobharthan, is a very difficult time for all of us," said Emlik. "We need the guidance of one who can see beyond all that we can see. If there are things that I should know, things you may have seen, I beg you, not just as your father, but as leader of this settlement, to tell them to me."

She walked away from him again and looked towards the mountains. For several moments she was silent, but then she spoke.

"I have seen things in the night, things that trouble me greatly." She paused again, mustering her courage. Her father had turned towards her, knowing in his heart the great effort that she was making for him. He knew too that he should not interrupt; that to stop her now would make the effort even more painful for her at a later time.

"A time of great danger for our people is approaching. It will be when —"

All of a sudden, there was much hustle and bustle behind them in the settlement and Orla came running and shouting, interrupting Sobharthan.

"Emlik! Emlik!" she screamed. "Come quickly, come quickly, it's Deirbhile. She is in trouble on the mountain!"

As she neared her husband, Orla's talk became less frantic, though her sense of urgency was every bit as strong. "Thor has returned with this in his mouth," she said, holding a piece of Deirbhile's sheepskin clothing in her hand.

Emlik turned. The telling of Sobharthan's vision would have to wait. She would not be spared the pain of a second telling after all. Emlik rushed towards Orla.

"Where is she? Where is she?" he demanded.

"At the place of the Great Standing Stones," said Orla, handing him the black-headed metal spear which Cneasán had given him last winter.

"Relco, Suibhne, come!" demanded Emlik, as he headed towards the mountain. They grabbed their weapons and followed him. Orla watched as her men-folk went towards the grey hills. Sobharthan came to her mother's side and squeezed her arm.

"Don't worry, Mother, this time they will be safe."

Deirbhile had gone into the hills to make an offering at Alyana's burial place. By now, each and every member of the camp had been shown a safe route to the Standing Stones, thereby avoiding any contact with the Barbey. It was a secret passageway above the caves of Aillwee Mountain. This was the route which the men took now.

As they neared the Great Standing Stones, they could see Deirbhile lying prostrate on one of the lime-stone clints of the Burren's surface. They approached with caution. There was no sign of any other being, animal or human. Immediately, Suibhne and Relco emptied their sheepskin quivers of their arrows and, folding them, placed them as a cushion under Deirbhile's head. She had a nasty bruise on the right side of her forehead. Emlik, who had proceeded in haste to the nearby well, the water of which was known amongst his people to have special powers, returned now and was wetting her forehead. Slowly her eyes opened and she smiled as she recognised the faces of those above her. She tried to get up, but Emlik put his hand against her shoulder.

"No," he said. "Rest a little longer. There is no hurry."

Deirbhile lifted her hand to her forehead and felt the spot where she had been injured.

"Something struck you, Deirbhile?" said Suibhne. Suibhne's mind was filled with thoughts of what had happened to his own son not so long ago.

"Yes," she said. "It was when I went between the Standing Stones and into the chamber." Tears were mounting in her eyes and her upset was plainly visible to the men.

"Easy, Deirbhile," said Relco. He rested his hand on her head and gently stroked her hair.

Emlik and Suibhne went to the chamber to see if there was anything which might explain the situation.

"Relco," called Emlik. "Come here."

Relco gently rearranged the quivers beneath his sister's head and then entered the chamber.

"Look," said Suibhne.

At the backing stone, the large bronze pot in which the mixed dusts of Alyana's and Knapper's bodies had been placed was overturned. There was no sign of the golden torcs and pins which Mánla had placed inside the pot. Gone, too, was the golden collar, that of Gleninsheen, which Cneasán had passed on to Emlik and which he, in turn, had brought here to please the good god, Daghda.

"They are all gone," said Deirbhile, who had got to her feet and had made her way back to the entrance of the chamber.

"Sit down, Deirbhile, child," said Emlik, holding her by the shoulders and easing her back into a seated position on the limestone floor.

"I was in the tomb," she blurted, "placing the bronze headband which I had made as an offering to the Daghda, when a shadow passed across the backing stone." She was upset as she told her story, but not so badly that, with a little encouragement, she could not continue.

"Yes?" said Relco. "There was someone there?"

"Yes, I turned around and there before me was a tall, dark man, with limbs of great strength." Again she sobbed with the memory of this upset and again Relco comforted her.

"It is all right, Deirbhile, there is no danger now."

She composed herself and then continued. "At first I saw his feet and then my eyes travelled up his body to his chest, and then . . ." She sobbed again.

"Yes?" said Suibhne.

"And then , . ." Now she sobbed violently and Emlik held her in his arms, gently patting her on the back and assuring her that she was safe. Gradually her sobbing eased, then stopped entirely, and she dried the tears from her cheeks.

"And then to his head," she said quite bluntly, bracing herself within so as to hold her courage as she said this.

She sobbed a little more now, but with nothing like the violence of her earlier upset.

"Yes?" said Suibhne, who in his mind had thought that, perhaps, the one whom Deirbhile had seen was also the one responsible for Fearghal's death.

Deirbhile steeled herself and spoke very directly. "He had the head of a black goat." And, having said this, she slumped into her father's arms, fully drained of all energy.

"The head of a black goat?" said Relco, looking at the others in bewilderment. "A human with the head of a goat! It is not possible."

"She has been greatly frightened," said Suibhne, "and when one is afraid, the mind can be the maker of many imaginings. She will be fine after she has slept a while."

Relco nodded approval of Suibhne's utterance. But Emlik made no comment. He pondered what she had said. Deirbhile, like Sobharthan, was quiet by nature. She was gentle and, though she did not have the brightness of her sister or her brother, she was, perhaps, the steadiest of the three.

They turned the pot upright again and scooped as many of the scattered ashes as they were able back inside it. There was nothing that they could do about the pieces of gold that had been taken. Even the head-band, which Deirbhile had specially made for this visit to Alyana's grave, was gone.

The three men took turns at carrying Deirbhile on their way back to the camp. In the secrecy of their minds, each combed through the details of what she had told them. Their thoughts and the reasoning in their thoughts differed as does night from day but, as there is no day without the night, nor night without the day, so too there was a connection in their thoughts. Relco, the young and daring warrior, thought of seeking out this man whom Deirbhile had described and of doing battle with him. Suibhne's greatest wish was to avenge the cruel death of his only son and, if that meant engaging the one who had inflicted the blow on Deirbhile, then so be it.

And Emlik. Emlik, the wise one. Emlik, the father. Emlik, the leader of his people. Always the leader. He could not think of battle or of vengeance; only of the safety of his people — this was his duty. When the blood ran hot in torrents through the bodies of the others, tempting them to battle, Emlik's blood was cool. It tempered the thoughts in his mind, telling him, above all else, what should *not* be done. What he *should* do, he did not quite know. He would speak again with Sobharthan.

6

Sobharthan's Illness, Fiachra's Secret, Pursuit, Treachery

Deirbhile recovered from her mishap quite quickly. Sobharthan, however, who on the same day had begun to reveal some of her visions to her father, was taken badly later that night. It seemed that, in her effort to tell of what she saw, she had been drained of all her energy and had fallen ill due to exhaustion of the mind. For many months, she lay in bed and had to be attended to by Orla and Deirbhile.

Emlik felt quite guilty about Sobharthan's illness because he knew that he had pressed her to tell him of her visions and he felt that, but for this, she would not be ill. It was a relief to him when, in midsummer, as the green crops of the fields stretched themselves and began to ripen, that Sobharthan had begun again to walk about the settlement. There was a brightness in her eyes that had been absent for some time and she had begun to talk in a much more positive fashion again.

And so, Emlik had resolved that, no matter what might happen, he would not raise the issue of troubles with her again. She was too tender of age to carry such weight. Besides, Frayika's marriage to Fiachra was to happen soon and he felt that their attention should be given to making that occasion one of great joy and happiness. After the trials they had endured since the Feast of Samhain, they were entitled to some revelry.

Frayika, these times, was radiant with the joys of love. Daily, she busied herself in preparation for her marriage. Fiachra's visits to the camp were much more regular now. He had come to know the ways of the family at Loch Reasc and had been trusted with their plans and secrets. They seemed so suited to each other: she, blue-eyed and blonde, while he, by contrast, was dark; she, vivacious and outgoing, he, a quieter, more silent type. He was tall and all were at one that he was handsome also. All agreed that, in both looks and temperament, they were perfectly suited to each other.

Very soon the time would come for all at Loch Reasc to meet Fiachra's people. Even Frayika had not met them yet! Fiachra, they knew, was from the south, far from the settlement at Loch Reasc. He had pointed out that in winter the elements did not afford the chance to his people to come and meet Frayika's family; and in the summer, work with the animals and the crops did not allow the time. Even when he himself would come, he would stay for many nights at a time, and when he'd leave they knew they might not see him again until the new moon came to the sky.

Harvest time had come and, when it would pass,
Fiachra and Frayika would marry. Sobharthan had, in
the course of the summer, fully regained her strength.
One night, during this time, when all in Loch Reasc
rested, Sobharthan came to her parents' hut. Orla and
Emlik were not sleeping. They had been talking of the
marriage plans.

"Who's there?" asked Orla, when she heard a noise
outside.

"It is I, Mother — Sobharthan," and she poked her
head in through the opening in the skins.

"Oh, Sobharthan, *a stór*! You gave us a bit of a
fright!" said her mother.

"Come in, come in," said Emlik, and he rose from
the bed of hay and threw back the skins at the front of
their hut, allowing the stars of the night to look at
them. While Sobharthan sat beside her mother, Emlik
began to rekindle the embers just outside the hut.
Soon a fire was burning and they seated themselves
around it.

"Can you not sleep, Sobharthan? Is it the excitement of Frayika's marriage?" her mother asked.

Sobharthan looked at her mother, then at her
father, and then she lowered her head to speak. "Yes,
Mother, I cannot sleep."

"Well, now you have company," said Emlik,
laughing at what he thought to be a witty comment.
But Sobharthan did not laugh or even smile.

"I am troubled," she said. "I fear for Frayika."

Orla and Emlik looked at each other, afraid that

perhaps, after all her improvement over the Summer, Sobharthan was suffering a relapse.

"What are you saying, Sobharthan, *a chroí*? What is it that you are afraid of?"

"I have great doubts about Fiachra, Mother."

Orla seemed a little exasperated now. "Doubts, love? What do you mean? He is a wonderful man. Look how happy Frayika is, and he is —"

"No, Orla," interrupted Emlik. "Let her speak." He turned then to his daughter. "Tell us of these doubts you have, Sobharthan."

She looked at her father. Always the strong one. Always prepared to listen.

"Why have we not met his people? What do we know of them? What do we even know of Fiachra himself, except for what he tells us?"

"Don't be silly, child! He's —" Again Emlik stretched his arm towards Orla, to silence her.

"Say what is on your mind, child," he said.

Sobharthan was gathering herself to speak. *She* had come to her parents this time. Emlik had not forced her to tell of what she saw. Within herself, she knew that she must make known what had come to her in a vision.

"Fiachra is not from the far south."

"What are you saying, Sobharthan!" exclaimed Orla.

Again Emlik prepared to silence Orla. But Sobharthan, seeing that what she knew must now be clearly stated, spoke before him.

"He is of the Barbey."

"What!" said Emlik, visibly shocked.

"Don't be ridiculous, child! He is from the south," her mother said, challenging the wisdom of her daughter.

Sobharthan looked at both of them. She knew the shock that she had dealt them with this news, but she also knew it was important that they believe her. Calmly, yet unflinchingly, she spoke again. "He is of the Barbey. It has come to me in a vision some time ago."

"But why didn't you speak of this before? Are you sure? Perhaps it is not a true vision," said Emlik, trying now to find an answer other than that which Sobharthan was saying to them. But his protestations were born of frustration, not of doubt. He knew his daughter well and, deep inside, he knew how much it must have taken for her to say what she had said. Quietly now, he accepted it. "Why didn't you tell us this before?" he asked again. This time his manner was quieter and more composed.

"I tried. I almost did tell you — the day that Deirbhile was injured at the place of the Standing Stones."

Emlik reflected. Of course, that was the day that Sobharthan was speaking of her visions. And then she was ill. And all this time she had had to carry the weight of this knowledge in her heart. Emlik threw his arms around his daughter and hugged her tightly.

"But how are we to know? What are we to do?"

asked Orla, seeing that Emlik had accepted the truth of Sobharthan's account and fearing, at the same time, the effect that news of this would have on Frayika. She would be devastated.

"He must be followed," announced Sobharthan, boldly. "The next time he leaves Loch Reasc to return to his own people, he must be followed."

"You are right, Sobharthan. You are right. We must follow him," said Emlik. "I am glad that you have told us this. It is best, I think, not to say anything to Frayika until we find out for sure."

Orla herself, having seen Emlik's definite belief in what Sobharthan had said, now believed her daughter also. She came to her and hugged her. "You have carried a great burden in your heart for a long time, my love," she said. "But now you are rid of it and you have been right to tell us what you have seen. Go now and sleep."

Sobharthan returned to her bed and Emlik and Orla to theirs, but not one of them slept that night, thinking of what was to be done.

Some days later, as evening neared, Fiachra, who had been at Loch Reasc since the old moon had entered its final quarter, was preparing to leave. It had been difficult for Emlik and Orla to conceal what they had learned. They bore their secret until he had gone and, when he was some distance from the camp, Emlik and

Relco followed. They were careful to stay well back so as to avoid him seeing them. Every now and then, Fiachra would stop and look around, almost as if he feared there might be someone in pursuit. He led them into the fertile valley that would take them to the twisting hill, which they knew as *Cornán na Nathrach* — The Snake's Curl.

"But why are we following him?" Relco asked his father.

Emlik and Orla had decided that nothing would be said to any of the others while Fiachra was in the camp. Now, as Relco was with him in tracking Fiachra, Emlik felt that it was right to tell him what they had come to know.

"Sobharthan has learned in a vision that Fiachra is of the Barbey."

"What!" exclaimed Relco in amazement. Then, composing himself and thinking a little on what he had just been told, he asked, "Is it true?"

"We will soon find out, my son."

They passed Lios an Rú, the settlement of Fearchú and Raithnika, continuing at a safe distance behind Fiachra. Still Fiachra looked back occasionally and, at times, Emlik and Relco had to duck into the long, lush grass to hide themselves from his gaze.

When, finally, Fiachra reached the top of the Snake's Curl, he stopped and again looked back down the valley. So as not to be detected, Emlik and Relco squeezed in tightly against a tree at the final twist of the track. Through the fern that stood around the tree, they saw Fiachra suddenly leave the track above and bound into the fields. Quickly, they mounted the final paces of the hill and, once on top, they looked across the fields. Fiachra was doubling back, quickly making his way through the long grass at the extremity of the half-cut meadow. There was no mistaking where he was heading.

"So, Father, it is true! Sobharthan's vision was accurate."

"Yes, indeed, though I had little doubt," said Emlik as his eyes followed Fiachra. "Now," he said, turning to his son, "we must follow and try to get as close to their camp as possible."

Relco looked anxious. Emlik saw the worry in his face and, not knowing that the younger man's anxiety was actually for him, the elder tried to give his son heart.

"Don't worry, my son. There is no danger as long as we keep our distance."

Night was closing in as Emlik and Relco crossed the outer walls of Cahermore. They looked back towards the Snake's Curl and, in places along the valley, they could see the night fires of many smaller settlements. They must be careful. They could not be sure that some of these smaller settlements were not of the Barbey. As they reached the main wall, they pressed their backs against it. They could feel each other's heartbeat against the rock and they breathed heavily. There was no entry to the camp from this side and they could not follow Fiachra to the front.

"We will have to climb the wall," said Emlik.

Relco looked at him and then they both looked above their heads. It was the height of three men.

"I have an idea," said Relco and, without waiting to explain, he took the three short-handled hunting knives which he carried in his belt. He dug one in hard between two stones, near to the base of the wall; the second, he put at the level of his chest and then, using the first two as steps, he sank the third higher up again.

"Give me your knife, Father," he said, as he stood where the second had been inserted. His father threw him up the knife and Relco, now standing on the third and gripping where he could between the spaces in the stones, drove the fourth knife in, making a final step. He eased his eyes above the level of the top layer of stones, looked right, then left, and then back down towards his father.

"It's safe. No one in sight," he whispered.

Emlik now mounted the steps which Relco had created and grabbed the outstretched arm of his son, to take him from the final support on to the top of the wall. Now they could hear voices from the camp. There were hazel bushes between them and the living area of the settlement. They crouched and moved quickly into the bushes, lying on their bellies, one behind the other. Once again, as at the outer wall, they could feel their hearts beating hard against the earth.

"Stay close," whispered Relco, who led the crawl amongst the hazels. Emlik, who perhaps should have had his full attention on what they were about, could not but think of how, when he was Relco's age, his own father had also begun to let him take the lead in things. More and more, he knew that he would yield to age and surrender his authority to his son.

Relco had come to a halt now and Emlik, using arms and legs against the earth, pulled himself along-side his son. He firmly clutched the back of the younger man's forearm, squeezing it, letting him know that he was proud of his courage and his care.

"Look," said Relco, nodding in the direction of the inner settlement.

Beyond the hazel bushes, seated by the campfire, was Fiachra, facing in their direction. Though thin of leaves at this time of year, the density of the bushes concealed them perfectly from Fiachra's vision and yet, the narrow spaces between the shoots gave Emlik and Relco a full view of those around the campfire. Two large black dogs lay, belly-down, beside the fire and there was movement in and out of huts at various spots within the settlement.

"What news do you bring us of Loch Reasc?" asked the man who sat across the fire from Fiachra. He was dark of hair and the broadness of his back suggested he was big when standing.

"They are harvesting every day from early morning and their store will be plentiful."

"And your marriage, Fiachra? They still suspect nothing?"

"Nothing at all, Duarcán, my sister," he answered.

Then all three laughed heartily.

Emlik and Relco looked at each other. Their noses almost touched in the tightness of the space. "His sister!" exclaimed Emlik. "Had he not told Frayika that he had no sister?"

They looked back towards the campfire. The one nearest to them now stood. He was, indeed, a big man, dressed in the skins of a leader. Still they could only see his back.

"What of the fools at Ballyallaban?" he asked. "Are they often in Loch Reasc these times?" He sat again.

"Hardly ever, now that it is harvest time, Dubhán."

Again Relco and Emlik looked at each other. So this was the Dubhán of whom they had heard! Emlik remembered now how readily, that night at Ballyallaban, Fiachra had known Dubhán's name, and how he had shut up again as soon as he had announced it. Things were beginning to explain themselves. Emlik moved forward a little to better hear what Dubhán was saying.

"Your sister and I have spent much time discussing —"

Suddenly, one of the dogs began to growl, a long, gnarled growl that seemed to roll up from his innards. The second dog now growled also and, as he did, the first stood and his growl became a bark. He barked in the direction of the bushes. Now both dogs were standing, barking, and Fiachra and Dubhán, whose speech was interrupted, rose to their feet.

"Let's go," whispered Emlik urgently.

They turned and, with skill, they worked their knees and elbows at great speed to take them back towards the high wall. In the background they could hear much shouting in the camp and the barking of the dogs had grown far louder. As they neared the edge of the hazel bushes, two of the Barbey guards ran towards each other from opposite ends of the wall.

"Wait," said Emlik, raising his hand a little to caution his son from rushing out. They stopped now, just inside the bushes and looked out at the two Barbey on the wall. The bearded clansmen both held torches which they stretched out over the perimeter of the wall, trying to see if there was any movement beyond the fort.

"The one on the left is mine, Father," whispered Relco. Emlik looked at him. The light from the torches made the shadows of the hazel twigs dance in his son's face.

"I suppose that that means the one on the right is mine then," said Emlik, smiling.

They laughed a half-laugh and clenched each other by the hand. They lifted their heads a fraction, just like a fox immediately before the pounce, and then surged forward. Neither of the Barbey knew anything of the oncoming rush until they were swept straight off the wall. They fell onto the vertical stones which were strewn outside the wall, intended to make footing difficult for any likely attackers. Both Emlik and Relco were cushioned as they fell heavily on top of the guards. The two Barbey were killed outright. Immediately, father and son doused the lighted torches which their victims had carried.

"Into the long grass and lie low," said Emlik, and they headed deep into the uncut end of the meadow.

Already, the rumpus within the stone fort seemed distant from them now. It had, they thought, abated quite quickly. No one, other than the two they had swept down off the wall, had come to check the back of the settlement.

They lay there for some time, then finally decided it was safe to make their way back home. They could hear no noise whatsoever from Cahermore at this stage.

"They must be sleeping," whispered Relco, as their heads appeared, like two stoats at a stone wall, above the long grass.

"Yes, all is quiet now," said Emlik, "but, just to be safe, we will travel back across the mountain to the front of Cahermore. It will leave no tracks."

They climbed the limestone rock onto the back of Aillwee Mountain and travelled a good distance to the east before facing north again. It was quite dark, but the clearness of the sky and the white-grey limestone helped their footing.

Now they were on familiar ground and were nearing the passageway through the rock at the back of the caves. As they began to descend the passageway and were getting close to the mouth of the main cavern, a black poc goat of the mountain rushed from the darkness and stood out on a large flat slab.

"Wait, wait," said Emlik, spreading his arm across his son's chest. "We have had enough troubles this night without inviting any more."

The goat held his head high, arrogantly, and surveyed the terrain in all directions. He lifted his head even higher now and, as they looked, the hairy meigeall under his chin fell in strands against the yellow of the moon. He bleated a long announcement that made its way out into the clear night air, and it was followed by the hollow sound of hooves against the rock.

Goats of all descriptions — a hundred, maybe more — appeared on precipices all along the mountain. The black goat bleated again into the night and the others answered in an unsettling cacophony. A final declaration from the leader, and he bolted down the mountainside, followed by the others. Soon the clanking of the hooves against the stone had stopped and the goats disappeared from view.

"All right, they are gone," said Emlik. They breathed a little more easily now and moved out from the closeness of the rock, which danger had made them favour. They hastily made for the foot of the mountain and crossed the fields that took them to Loch Reasc.

To their surprise, all at Loch Reasc were still seated around the campfire. As Emlik and Relco entered the settlement, Orla rose and ran to greet her husband.

"What news?" she whispered, as they walked

together towards the centre of the camp.

"It is true," he answered.

Orla stopped her husband now before reaching the others at the campfire.

"I have told Frayika of our suspicions, so she has been prepared for the worst," said Orla.

"You have done well, then."

Emlik and Relco sat in around the campfire and they related the findings of the night. There was a strong bond of closeness amongst the family members at Loch Reasc as they listened to their leader. Even Frayika had steeled her nerve, realising that it was better that she know now of Fiachra's deceit than to have the Barbey come upon them by stealth.

They discussed openly what they should do when next Fiachra would come to the camp. There were suggestions born of anger: he should be killed, some said. After all, he had spied on them and had taken their secrets to the Barbey. Who was to know what they knew and did not know of the people at Loch Reasc?

But others were more moderate, suggesting that it would be sufficient to send him on his way, letting him know that they knew of his deceit. As happens when there are many people gathered with a difference of opinion, the discussion around the campfire intensified. More was said and less was heard. Then Sobharthan spoke and all but she were silent.

"There is no need to wonder what should be said

or done with Fiachra. He will never again enter this camp *alone*."

They looked at one another. All had noticed the emphasis which Sobharthan had placed on the word 'alone'. Her father, being leader of these people, spoke their minds.

"Sobharthan, you say that Fiachra will never again enter this camp alone. Is there something else that we should know?"

He phrased his question carefully, hoping to live true to his resolve not to pressurise his daughter.

"*I have seen it at the back of my eyes, where the seer pierces the darkness of the inner mind,*" she said. "*It will be the time of darkness, when Earth and Moon and Sun are one. They will come out of the rock, breathing fire and iron against us and* SHE *will rule their minds. And there will be destruction.*"

Sobharthan slumped forward now, her long, dark hair reaching to the ground. She was exhausted.

"What does it mean?" asked Relco. "How can the earth and moon and sun be one?"

"Who will come with fire and iron? Is it the Barbey?" asked another.

"Who is this 'She' who will rule their minds?" Orla asked.

But Sobharthan did not try to answer their every question. She let the others tire themselves with talk and, when they had done, she spoke.

"I do not know. I only see, but I cannot understand,"

she said. There was great listlessness in her speech.

Before another summer had passed, their questions would be answered.

7

Slaughter, Emlik's and Relco's Confession,
Interpreting the Prediction,
Readying for Battle

Next morning, as the sun crept over the top of the mountain, all but Emlik slept. It had been almost light when they had gone to their beds and, were it not for Thor's incessant barking, Emlik too would still be sleeping.

"Lie down, Thor," he shouted from the hut. This did not quieten the dog. Indeed, if anything, his barking grew louder and more alarming. Eventually, Emlik realised that sleep and Thor were doing battle and that sleep would be the vanquished. He threw off the fleece covering and came to the opening in his tent.

"Will you be quiet, you —"

Emlik stopped dead in his speech and, parting the skins of the tent, saw a huge black cloud of smoke rising from the distant trees. He thought a second, cleared the sleep out of his eyes and then looked again. It was Ballyallaban! He darted back into the hut.

"Orla, Orla, get up, get up! It's Ballyallaban.

There's a fire, there's a fire!" he shouted. Orla, who was sleeping heavily, was having difficulty awakening.

"Orla, Orla, Ballyallaban has been burnt," shouted Emlik frantically, as he shook her to a fully wakened state. Then he ran out of the tent, shouting for Relco. His son was quickly at his side.

"Sound the alarm. Get them out of their huts," instructed Emlik.

Relco did as he was told and, just as one and then another, then yet another still, sleepily emerged from the many huts within the settlement, Cneasán and his people, or what remained of them, appeared beyond the outskirts of the settlement. They were walking slowly, some propping up the injured as they came. Others carried women and children, burnt and wounded, in their arms. A wagon, drawn by oxen, was filled with bodies, covered red in their own blood. Their arms and legs, dangling through the openings on the sides of the laden wagon, caressed the tops of the grass as they drew nearer to the camp.

"Oh no! Oh no!" cried Emlik, as he looked out in anguish at his approaching kinsmen. He went forward to them, gathering momentum as he moved. Orla and the others followed.

As Cneasán saw them coming, he halted his own people and waited for his friend's arrival. His eyes and those of Emlik met.

"The Barbey," said Cneasán. There was no need for more.

The injured were taken in and cared for. Beds were readied, animals moved, huts were emptied and then refilled with the half-torn bodies of their Ballyallaban kinsfolk. Throughout the day the wagon was emptied and the dead, as had now become the Celtic custom, were buried in one huge black pit beyond the outer fencing of the settlement. There was mourning all day long and cries of sadness went on deep into the night. It was a black day, the blackest that any could remember.

Cneasán, being their chieftain, tended to his people the whole day long. His grief was great. His own wife, Mánla, had fallen in the battle. Mánla of the gentle heart, the kindly smile, the noble face — all the thoughts of loveliness that heightened the ache within Cneasán's heart seemed to tantalise his mind now. The first time ever he had seen her, so many summers ago; the joys they shared; the sorrows they had carried, one for the other; their children and now their children's children; his wisdom, her kindness; his strength, her gentleness. Now it was gone and he was halved, even less than halved: he was nothing.

It was night. The stars glittered in the clear sky overhead and Cneasán, seated by the campfire, looked across the settlement of Loch Reasc, beyond to where his Mánla lay beneath the darkness of the earth. He imagined her still breathing, still smiling. Maybe he would awaken and find that it was all a dream; Mánla lying beside him, sleeping, contented in her rest.

"Take heart, my friend. You have done all that you can do and more than any man." Cneasán felt the strength of Emlik's hand upon his shoulder as his younger friend spoke those words of comfort to him. The yellow flames danced in Cneasán's eyes, their reflection thickening the tears that rested against his lower eyelids. All was at peace now. The wounded lay in the many huts around them. The dead slept deeply in the blackness of the soil. All was quiet save the gentle talk of those around the fire.

"I don't know why," said Cneasán, "why, after all that time of no involvement, no contact, no troubles between us, they should have come upon us with such savagery in the darkness of the night."

Both Relco and Emlik knew what was in each other's thoughts as Cneasán spoke. Though they had not discussed it, it had filled their minds throughout the day as they buried half-burnt bodies and tended to the wounded. Perhaps the cause of the Barbey's anger had been their incursion into Cahermore just the night before. Their sense of guilt was mounting. Though Cneasán continued his musings, they really did not hear him. Father and son looked across the firelight and, through their eyes, they spoke to each other.

"Maybe we know what has caused their anger, Cneasán." It was Emlik who had taken the responsibility of speaking.

"What do you mean?" asked Cneasán, becoming more attentive to the others seated around the fire.

"Maybe we can shed some light on why this evil happened to your people."

The chieftain of Loch Reasc went on to tell, in detail, of the visions which had come to Sobharthan and of how both he and Relco had followed Fiachra to the Cahermore, that night's events, the alerting of the Barbey and the alarm within their camp. As he spoke, Emlik, as too did Relco in his silence, feared that once their story had been told, Cneasán would blame them for the massacre that had befallen his clan. Once finished, all eyes were fixed on Cneasán. There was a tension in the silence. Time seemed long. Then, finally, Cneasán spoke. "If this was the cause of the Barbey's anger," he said, "then it has only come before some other cause."

Those in the gathering looked across at one another. There was relief in every face. Half-smiles broke out and a growing banter dismissed the silence, and with it, all its awkwardness and tension. Emlik reached his arm out towards his friend and, as they tightly grasped each other's forearm, both minds at once went back to that first night when they had formed their bond of friendship.

Cneasán's mind was lucid now. There were others of his clan who had survived the ordeal and who would still be in need of his wisdom and leadership.

"The visions," he said, directing his attention towards Sobharthan, "are they now fulfilled?"

"They must be," said Relco enthusiastically. The exuberance of his youth, mixed with the relief that

Cneasán had not blamed him and his father for the tragedy at Ballyallaban, fired his speech. Sobharthan, in her quietness, allowed her brother the briefness of his enthusiasm.

"I cannot be sure," she said. "There is much that I cannot interpret."

"But," said Relco, again revealing his youthful certainty that the visions were fulfilled, "the vision that Fiachra is of the Barbey has been confirmed." He stopped now a second, remembering that Frayika was in their company. He looked towards her, half in apology for his lack of sensitivity. She hung her head. She too, though totally without reason, had felt a guilt for what had happened to the people at Ballyallaban. Relco, now somewhat less confident, continued.

"And it must be that last night's destruction is the fulfilment of the second vision." He looked at the others and the signs of approval of his interpretation from those around the fire renewed his belief that he was right and tempted him towards his youthful over-confidence again. "Can't you see?" he said. "'Coming out of the rock' is the Barbey coming out of the stone fort of Cahermore, and 'Breathing fire and iron' is the death and destruction that they have caused."

The assembly, in general, seemed to agree that Relco's understanding of the vision was correct. Frayika, who was seated beside Sobharthan, still held her head low and was filled with feelings of embarrassment and guilt. Emlik however, despite his many summers in the land of the Celts, had kept that strong trait of coolness and of objective thought that was the hallmark of his Nordic fathers. He spoke. "It would seem that all that Relco says is true."

Relco swelled with pride at what he all too hastily took to be his father's approval of his reading of the situation.

"But," said Emlik, deflating any danger of over-arrogance in his son, "what of that part of the vision which talks of earth and moon and sun being one?"

He looked to Relco. His son simply shrugged his shoulders and looked across to Sobharthan.

"I do not know," said Sobharthan, "but I feel that if so incredible a thing did happen, then we would surely know of it." This too seemed to gain the approval of those present.

"I do not believe that the second of the visions has been fulfilled," she said emphatically. "I think that there is more to come."

Samhain was fast approaching and all agreed that it was best that Cneasán and his people should winter at Loch Reasc. Their harvest at Ballyallaban had been destroyed and there was little sense in returning to the settlement until Imbolc smiled again. As the wounded regained their strength, they assisted in the final stages of the gathering in and storing of the harvest. The earth, if not much else, smiled upon their fortunes and the harvest was bountiful, yielding ample food for all and as much again to spare.

Fearchú and Raithnika had came to Loch Reasc as soon as they had heard of events at Ballyallaban. It was only then that they too learned of Sobharthan's more recent visions. Raithnika's heart opened to her sister when she heard of Fiachra's deceit. She was a great comfort to Frayika at that time and, in a strange way, this adversity rekindled the strong bond which had existed between them in their childhood.

While Fearchú returned to Lios an Rú to attend to the final stages of the harvest there, Raithnika stayed on at Loch Reasc for some time, helping with the wounded and enjoying her sister's company. When the time came for her to rejoin her husband, Frayika went with her. Along with them they also took some of the children who had been orphaned in the Barbey attack. It was felt that it would be good for them to be taken from the reminders of the ordeal they had endured. Besides, at Lios an Rú there were Raithnika's children, Saoirse and Fionnán, not to mention those of the others in the settlement; this would provide opportunity for play and distraction. It was agreed that they would all convene again to celebrate the Feast of Samhain at the settlement in Loch Reasc.

Meanwhile, at Loch Reasc, while by day they busied themselves with the crops, the early part of the nights were spent around the campfire, telling tales, talking of the hunt and of fishing, the latter being a practice which Emlik and his people had introduced to their Celtic brothers when first they came to those parts. One night, after the younger ones had left the campfire for their beds, the talk turned to the days that lay ahead. It was impossible to forget all that had happened. The need to be prepared for the very worst was all important. Sobharthan's visions were discussed, they were combed and pondered time and time again. A decision was made that some of the men should devote their time to ensuring that the weaponry within the camp was in perfect order.

"If anything should happen," said Cneasán, "we don't want to be unprepared as we were at Ballyallaban."

"You are right, Cneasán. We must be ready for every possibility," said Emlik.

Emlik shifted his gaze to his son. "Relco," he said, "I want you and Suibhne here to take charge of the sharpening of all stone weapons in the camp."

Suibhne, who was seated near to Emlik, nodded his willingness to work with Relco in this effort.

"Cneasán and I will take charge of the weapons with heads of metal. Everything will be readied," said Emlik.

"What if there is no attack?" asked Iarla, one of Cneasán's kinsmen.

"If there is no attack, Iarla," said Cneasán, and he paused to look at the ambered faces gathered about the fire, "then we will have the sharpest of weapons when we hunt the wild boar once the fine weather comes again."

They had all waited anxiously to hear Cneasán finish his answer and, once said, they laughed with pleasure at the wisdom of his words.

"Let us hope, my friends, that that is the greatest use our weaponry will have," said Emlik.

"Agreed," said Cneasán.

"Agreed," repeated the others in unison. Then all fell into groups of conversation, discussing the various inputs they might make to ensure the successful completion of the tasks ahead.

The days that followed were days of great industry. Every spear and arrowhead, whether of stone or of metal, was laid out in a pile in the centre of the settlement. Those youngsters who had not gone to Lios an Rú with Raithnika and Frayika were given the task of separating stone from metal and arrowheads from spearheads; this would include them in the great communal effort, increase their awareness of the importance of defence and, if nothing else, would afford the adults the time necessary for the carrying out of their own roles.

The men and women travelled together in groups to where the hazel bushes grew, cut down branches and hauled them back into the settlement. Because this wood was both sturdy and pliant, it was perfect for the making of new shafts for the weapon heads. Suibhne and Relco ground the flint heads against their sharpened hand axes and, once ready, handed them on to other workers to fasten onto the treated shafts. Emlik and Cneasán did likewise with the metal implements and they had even forged some new metal axes which, even if not used for battle, would have many other uses both within and outside the settlement.

A further team of men now busied themselves erecting a fence inside the bushes at the perimeter of the settlement. Unlike Ballyallaban and Lios an Rú, there was no earthen bank or water-filled moat encircling the Loch Reasc camp. Up to now, there was never any need of such.

"The wattled fence will have to suffice for now," said Emlik, as he and Suibhne came to inspect the work.

"Hopefully it will not have to serve the purpose for which it is being erected," his comrade replied.

Two nights before the Eve of Samhain, all work had been completed. The harvest was entirely saved and stored; an arsenal of newly strengthened weapons was ready and intact; and the wattled fence within the bushes had been finished that very day.

"We have done well, my people," said Emlik. "Much work has been done in little time." There was a general rumble of satisfaction amongst the people of the camp.

"It is time now to rest," Emlik continued. "The Feast of Samhain is close at hand and its sacredness cannot be profaned. Let us be happy with our toil and with our efforts."

8

Samhain, Emlik's Address, The Final Vision,
The Fight, Good and Evil, Another Form

The Eve of Samhain had come at last. That morning, the people from Lios an Rú departed their camp, leaving behind only their dogs. With them, tied on two sturdy staffs and carried by men from the settlement, they bore a pig and a sheep that had been killed and readied especially for the feast. The shoulders of the carriers were red and sore by the time they reached Loch Reasc.

"You are welcome, friends," said Orla, as they entered the settlement.

Emlik had a special welcome for his sisters. He had not seen them since Raithnika had taken Frayika back with her to Lios an Rú. He embraced them fondly. The three of them had become even closer since Alyana's death. It was hard to believe that one whole summer, Samhain to Samhain, had passed since that tragic night. It had been a time of great turmoil. The death of Alyana and Knapper was only the start of what seemed to become a never-ending series of troubles: Fearghal's strange death in Moneen Valley; the attack on Deirbhile at the place of the Great Standing Stones;

Sobharthan's disturbing visions; Fiachra's cruel deceit and the Barbey's merciless attack on Ballyallaban. Never before had they experienced such a troubled time.

But things gone were gone. It was the Feast of Samhain: a time to bid farewell to things gone by; a time to rest, to restore oneself and to look forward to the new. Though there was still the unsettling business of Sobharthan's final vision and the uncertainty of whether or not it had been fulfilled, Emlik knew that Samhain was sacred — even to the Barbey. He also felt that, once it had passed and winter took hold, there would be no danger to them.

As night began to fall and the grey stone of the Burren hills to the east of the camp began to darken, the full moon of Samhain climbed slowly into the clear sky. A little later, the hard crisp bite of winter filled the air and its sharpness seemed to make the star-filled speckled carpet overhead even brighter than it otherwise might be. Even the hills now had lost that initial dullness of the onset of night and had, under the brightness of the lighted sky, regained their rugged greyness.

Inside the camp the gaiety had begun. Suibhne was amongst the young ones, helping to arrange activities. It was a time for children to celebrate their childhood. As in years gone by, they busied themselves with the many games that, for their fathers and their mothers before them, had made childhood speed away. For some of the children, their memory and their knowledge of the games they played the previous Samhain would make them organisers and leaders on this night. There was nothing different to any other Samhain, except that all those present had seen another summer pass.

The grown-ups, as was their habit, were seated about the fire. Again, the customary banter rang about the settlement. There was talk of the goodness of the harvest and of the newly started practice of fishing from rafts in the sea to the north of the settlements. Thoughts, however, soon turned to the summer that had passed.

"What of Fiachra?" asked Fearchú. "I presume he has not dared to show his face since his treachery at Ballyallaban."

"No, indeed," said Emlik, "we have seen nothing of him since that night."

"Good riddance to him too," said Relco. There was anger in the young man's voice.

"Now, Relco!" said Orla, tightening her lips as she looked across at her son. He knew it was his mother's way of rebuking him for having been so outspoken in Frayika's presence.

"It was a bad business and is best forgotten," said Emlik, trying, in his usual manner, to keep the conversation on an even keel.

"You are right, Emlik," said Cneasán. "It is a time for looking forward, not backward. A time for building and for thinking afresh."

Cneasán looked quite old this night. He was a man

of fifty summers now and no longer had the energy of youth. The ransack of Ballyallaban had taken its toll on him. Even Emlik could see the change in him. His face had greyed since Mánla's death. In some respects, Emlik likened his old friend's situation to that of his own mother, Alyana, after Relco had died. And yet, unlike Alyana's case, Cneasán's mind was still alert and active in many ways.

"When will work at Ballyallaban commence?" asked Suibhne, who had just joined the company at the fire, having finished his organising of the games amongst the young ones.

"As soon as winter passes and the first buds are to be seen on the trees, we will make a move," said Cneasán. "It will still leave us ample time to plant for the following harvest."

"There will be no shortage of help," said Raithnika, nodding in the direction of the young ones in the background.

"Yes," said Frayika, "we are blessed with many children, who will see our work continued long after we are gone."

All this time, Sobharthan, as was her wont, sat in silence between her father and her mother. To Emlik's other side sat Deirbhile. Emlik had lovingly placed an arm across each of his daughters' shoulders.

"Yes, indeed," he said, and he hugged both his daughters at the one time. "We are truly blessed with our children."

"To our children!" said Fearchú, raising his goblet.

"To our children!" the company responded.

The toast was drunk. As he lowered his goblet Fearchú asked, "What can you see ahead of us, Sobharthan?"

The young girl looked at Fearchú. Still, her deep, dark eyes held knowledge that she could not understand. She was an instrument of some power far greater than herself.

"I cannot see anything, Fearchú," she said.

Emlik, whose arms still held his daughters, could feel a tremble run through Sobharthan's body. Always he was concerned that she should not be overtaxed. Above all else, he did not wish that she should ever again suffer for the gift of insight which she had been given.

"Good, good," he said. "If there is nothing seen, then we must believe that it is because there is nothing to be seen."

Again he hugged his daughter to him and they understood each other: he, the need to shelter her and she, the need to be sheltered.

"Now, let us eat," said Emlik, and with this announcement he totally dismissed any other matters.

The children in the background took their cue from Emlik's words. They abandoned their games now and came to the circle of adults around the fire, squeezing themselves into the narrow spaces between their parents or their older brothers and sisters, and forcing the circle to become much wider in its welcome. The meat was carved, the meal eaten and the children quickly abandoned their new-found allegiance to the adults, preferring to return to the games that had earlier won their favour. Everything was as it had been the year before and the year before that again and further back than anybody present on that night could possibly remember.

Emlik stood. It was time to make his chieftain's address. Time to announce a welcome formally to his people, one and all. Only one full summer ago it had been Cneasán's duty to do so. He was filled with thoughts of all that had passed since last they celebrated Samhain. Alyana's face danced in his mind and forced tears into his eyes. He must be strong, he thought; he must be positive. Of course, he would have to speak of things that had happened in recent times, but they must not be laboured. He must generate hope amongst his people — hope and a belief in the future and in themselves. There was silence. Even the children had quietened again and had sat to listen to Emlik's words. Silence.

"My people, you are welcome here this Eve of Samhain."

He paused, allowing the gathering to murmur amongst themselves, as indeed they always did following the initial words of the chieftain's address. It was as if there was a need to do so in order to dispel that tension that always seemed to precede the speaker's opening words. They settled again.

"This is a time when . . ."

Emlik stopped. All eyes were fixed on him, but

his own eyes looked, in alarm, beyond the company and were fastened on Cappanawalla Mountain to the south. Strands of red and yellow light ran up his face and wove their way through the fairness of his hair. First Fearchú, then Cneasán and then Relco turned to look at the mighty mountain. Tongues of light, as if of fire, raced across its summit, almost as though they were driven by the wind. The men jumped up and quickly, too, the women and young ones were on their feet. The children seated in the background ran to the safety of the adults. Suibhne, who had turned to see what caused this light on Emlik's face, rushed towards him.

"What is it, Emlik, what is it?" asked Suibhne, frantically. There was danger in the panic apparent in his voice. Emlik grabbed him firmly by the upper arm, half in comfort, but half to let him know that it was his duty to remain calm.

"You must be strong, Suibhne — for the others," said Emlik, hoping that his kinsman could show his mettle when most it mattered. Suibhne could see the racing light in the pupils of Emlik's eyes. This was Samhain, when things of Nature passed out of the hands of Man. It was a time for courage. He sprang away from Emlik. The battle that he waged against his fear was written in his face. He would be as Emlik bade. He would be strong.

"Right," he said, "the older women and children into the huts." His manner was controlled and firm, the very traits his leader had hoped he would display.

With the help of Orla, Raithnika and Frayika, he began to steer the weaker of the kinsfolk towards the safety of cover.

"Cneasán, Fearchú, Relco!" called Emlik, summoning them to his side in the middle of the encampment. All four crouched onto their hunkers.

"What is it, Father? What is happening?" asked Relco, bemused and fearful of what was yet to come.

"I don't know," said Emlik. "I simply do not know."

The ground beneath them swirled in the kaleidoscope of colour created by the streams of light still sweeping over the top of the mountain. Patterns of red and yellow, green and purple, wove and danced within the settlement.

"We must try to get . . . " Emlik stopped. He could see Sobharthan standing at the southern end of the encampment, near to the new fencing which had been erected.

"Wait here," he said to the others, and he moved away from them. He came towards his daughter. She was looking at the distant mountain. The streams of colour ran like snakes across her body, causing shadows to caress her face and head. Emlik stood behind her and placed his hand on her shoulder.

"What is this, Sobharthan? What is this thing that is happening?" She did not turn to face him; she simply placed her hand upon her father's. Emlik could feel the coldness of her touch.

"I do not know, Father. It is something that is

beyond us, not something of this world."

This worried Emlik. His daughter seemed removed from him, not the usual Sobharthan who, despite her gift, could show more warmth and love than any normal child.

Suddenly, almost as if by decree, the racing light abated and the sky over Cappanawalla resumed its normal darkness. She turned to face her father and, as she did, a shrilling, high-pitched cry came from Moneen Mountain and pierced the night. Sobharthan's eyes lighted.

"The Animal!" she whispered. Her voice was tinged with fear. "The Goat!"

Both she and Emlik turned to face Moneen Mountain when, suddenly, a flash of lightning struck at the entrance to the settlement. In its light stood Fiachra. It flashed again and once again there stood Fiachra, laughing a mocking laugh. Emlik made to go at him, but Sobharthan placed her hand across him, indicating to him not to do so.

"No, he is not there," she said. "Do not be fooled."

Again the lightning flashed, but this time there was no sign of Fiachra. Already Relco and Fearchú were making for the spot where Fiachra had appeared. Again the Goat bleated its sinister cry into the clear night air.

"Look, look!" shouted Orla, running from one of the huts. As she spoke, she pointed to the sky. The moon had been full this night, but now a shadow was encroaching on it, taking from its roundness. They stood together and raised their eyes, watching the creeping darkness eat into the moon. It was not a cloud. Sobharthan walked out from them and the shadow that was creeping across the moon was cast upon her face.

"It will be the time of darkness, when Earth and Moon and Sun are one," she said. *"They will come out of the rock, breathing fire and iron against us and* SHE *will rule their minds. And there will be destruction."*

"It is the second vision!" said Cneasán and terror filled his eyes. "It is to be fulfilled! It is to be fulfilled!"

Again the bleat and then the lightning. And again and again. And in the place where Fiachra had stood, now there stood the Barbey in great number. When the lightning flashed again they surged into the camp, wielding spears and axes with great venom and torching the fence and the huts in which the women and children had taken refuge.

"Relco, Suibhne, get the weapons, get the weapons," screeched Emlik, as he moved, unarmed, in the direction of the huts. Anger had consumed him and, despite his lack of weaponry, he used his great strength to throw many of the marauding Barbey aside. In the distance, through the smoke, he could see the frame of Dubhán, leader of the Barbey, with Fiachra by his side. They were orchestrating the attack. Dubhán was dressed all in black, wearing full battle attire and a chieftain's head-dress.

"Father, catch!" shouted Relco, and he threw a spear and a hunting knife to him.

Already many of the women and children had been slain. Others had fled towards the perimeter fencing and were screaming and rolling in the grass, trying to douse the fire which had caught their clothing. The number of the Barbey appeared to be endless; for every one of Emlik's people, it seemed there were four or five of the invaders.

"Knock the fencing! Knock the fencing!" shouted Emlik.

Cneasán and his kinsman, Iarla, moved towards the centre of the settlement. They raised the huge log on which earlier they had sat and ran with it in the direction of the fence. Once there, they began to batter the fence with it, standing one behind the other, each lending all his weight to the effort.

Soon the fence began to yield to the pounding. It leaned outwards now, and two or three more charges would see it flattened to the ground. Some of the women, seeing the efforts of Cneasán and Iarla, had begun to steer the children in their direction. But Dubhán, too, had seen their progress. He directed Fiachra and a number of his men to attend to the situation and, just as Cneasán and Iarla made a final surge, they were swooped upon by the Barbey. They died instantly. Fiachra stood over Cneasán's body and grinned broadly in the direction of his leader, Dubhán.

The inside of the settlement was an inferno. Those still alive stepped on the bodies of their kinsfolk, as they tried to escape the viciousness of the Barbey. Any fortunate enough to make their way outside the fencing were quickly set upon and slaughtered. Fearchú, knowing that if Dubhán could be taken out the Barbey would become disheartened, was now engaging their leader in battle. Already he had seen the Barbey chieftain finish off the brave, but ageing Suibhne. He had fallen, clutching the skull that hung from Dubhán's belt, never knowing that it was that of his own son, Fearghal.

Fearchú, now, had got the upper hand on Dubhán. He pinned him to the ground and, while holding a hunting knife to his throat, was trying to push off the chieftain's head-dress. Suddenly, Fearchú's eyes bulged, as though emphasising the great effort he was making. A dark trickle of blood crept out from the corner of his mouth and his hands and arms were drained of all their strength. Slowly, he reached behind him and clutched the spear which had entered his back; he rolled off the Barbey leader. Fiachra stood above his sister's husband and reached down his hand, hauling Dubhán to his feet again.

They looked around. Of the people of Loch Reasc, only Emlik and Relco were still standing. Beyond the fence the Barbey hunted in packs, mercilessly finishing off the ones who had crawled outside the settlement. Relco's back was turned to them.

"Now is your chance," urged Dubhán. Fiachra did not hesitate. He surged forward, his spear held firm, and ran the son of Emlik through. And now there was but one.

Dubhán looked into the sky. The shadow on the

moon had inched its way and had, by now, almost
totally covered the ball of light. He laughed an evil
laugh and the brightness of the fire around him shone
in the darkness of his eyes. Far out on Aillwee
Mountain, the wild goat crowed its cry of victory.
Dubhán's head-dress was the hollowed head of one of
these mountain goats. He called back an answer to the
wild.

The dark chieftain turned to face Emlik. The final
victim. Dubhán's nostrils swelled with the smell of
vengeance. Fiachra was wrestling with the leader of
Loch Reasc. There was much for Emlik to avenge.
Everything. His sister's honour, his son, his wife, his
people. Both men were on their feet again. Emlik's
hands, fired by the frenzy that he felt within himself,
closed tightly on to Fiachra's neck. The younger man
fell to his knees, still firmly in Emlik's grip. Emlik
never dreamed that he could find such satisfaction in
the kill. It was an aspect of himself which he had
never known before. Then, stealing Emlik's moment
of revenge, a long shafted spear shot into Fiachra's
back and the Barbey warrior's resistance was over.
Emlik felt the sudden limpness of the body in his
grasp. He looked across the settlement and his eyes
met those of Dubhán, leader of the Barbey. Without
thinking, Emlik released his hold on Fiachra, letting
the body fall, facedown at his feet. He was confused.
He could not understand.

"You! But why?"

"Revenge is mine," said Dubhán, "not Fiachra's."

"What do you mean?"

Dubhán came forward to the middle of the settlement. As he did, the flames of the burning huts glittered in the golden collar which he wore around his neck. For the first time ever, Emlik held the vicious Dubhán in full view. The sight of the collar, coupled with the Barbey's head-dress, triggered a series of images in Emlik's mind: the attack on Deirbhile at the place of the Great Standing Stones; the man with the head of a goat; the golden collar; the upturned pots and desecration at Alyana's resting place.

Emlik's eyes reddened with rage. He could feel the veins pulsate in his head, heated by the rushing of the blood that coursed in anger through them.

"It was you!" exclaimed Emlik.

Dubhán threw his head back and, once again, he laughed in derision. Emlik was unable to contain himself. He rushed forward, knocking Dubhán to the ground. They scrambled, rolling violently this way and that, pressing each other's face into the hardness of the earth. First one, then the other seemed to have the upper hand. They moved at such speed that it was hard at times to tell how the contest went. Finally, the rolling stopped.

Dubhán now knelt across Emlik's chest, pinning the Loch Reasc chieftain to the ground. His hands reached for Emlik's neck and tightened round it. The downward pressure of the Barbey warrior gave him an advantage over his opponent. He squeezed tightly, causing Emlik's mind to wander in and out of semiconsciousness. Emlik could see the final remnant of the moon over Dubhán's shoulder — Dubhán's *left* shoulder. In that instant, the shadow finally blotted out its light and the memory of the struggle on the raft so many years before flashed into Emlik's mind. Dubhán, slowly and deliberately, reached his hand up to his head-dress and then whipped it off.

"I want you to know, Brother, by whom you have been vanquished."

Emlik looked up in amazement.

"Darkon!" he cried. He could not believe his eyes. "But why? Why the . . ."

As he spoke, he felt the sharp pain of Darkon's knife entering beneath his ribcage. The piercing sensation echoed right through Emlik's body causing him, at first, to writhe and squirm beneath his brother's weight. He was listless now, his mind increasingly in and out of consciousness. Above him, Darkon laughed and emitted the cry of the goat again and again.

It seemed to Emlik that, as Darkon laughed, his features began to change; he seemed half-goat now. Emlik tried to speak, but found he could no longer do so. Suddenly, the pain gripped all his inner organs at one time. His body heaved upwards, pivoted on his shoulders and his heels, and the chieftain of Loch Reasc emitted a final cry of surrender. And he was gone. Gone.

The black goat stood beside his brother's body. He lifted his head and crowed his message of victory out into the night. The noise of hooves against the distant limestone mountain was followed by a medley of bleated responses. Then the descent began. The sound of the hooves, chalkily chipping against the rock, grew louder and louder as, one by one, the mountain goats came to form a herd. Then, suddenly, there was silence. And then, as suddenly again, the goats stampeded into the settlement. They came from all sides, as wildly as had the Barbey, thundering into the camp and goring all the bodies strewn within the encampment. For many minutes, all inside the camp was a mass of wild, frenetic movement, heightened in its evil by the embers of the fire which, every now and then, were caught by the hooves of the frenzied goats and kicked high into the air.

Then Darkon, the Black Goat, summoned a halt. All the others gathered together in the centre of the settlement and looked to their leader. He bleated a message to his herd and, in response, they turned and left the camp. They were gone as quickly as they had come, leaving behind them their leader, Darkon, and the gored bodies of all who fell at Loch Reasc. Darkon had finally exacted his revenge.

But there was one who had not fallen, who could not fall, for it was in her nature that, in one form or another, she must live for all time. Darkon, now alone amongst the dead, felt a presence behind him. He turned slowly, the red, blood-dripping tips of his horns catching the light reflected from the embers of the fire. To the back of the camp stood the slight and solitary figure of a young girl. Her back was turned to the Goat. She raised her head to face the sky. Immediately the shadow that had caused the moon to hide its light moved quickly to one side. It was Sobharthan, the Blessed One. She had survived the massacre.

Sobharthan — daughter of Emlik; Emlik — son of Relco;
Relco — father of Darkon; Darkon — brother of Emlik;
Emlik — father of Sobharthan. Sobharthan — the Seer.
She turned slowly, for slowly turns The Circle.
And, like The Circle, there can be no end.

The young girl's eyes met those of the Goat. Dark on dark. Deep on deep. Black on black. Darkon inclined his head slightly to the side, bemused a little, searching quizzically the depth of Sobharthan's unsettling stare. To his amazement, her eyes began to lighten. The Seer's light, that filled her inner head with vision, turned outwards now. She looked at him, with eyes as bright as was the moon, staring deep into his mind. The strain he felt brought pain to Darkon's eyes. He broke the stare, no longer able to withstand the punishment she dealt. The Goat cowered away from her, backing, cringing, wanting to escape, but some-how, immobilised by this greater power. Unnerved, he backed on to the fire. The shock and suddenness of the heat forced his eyes to meet Sobharthan's again. She held her stare, transfixing Darkon and tying him where he stood amongst the embers. She steeled herself and watched him wilt before her, melting into the fire. At last, he emitted a cry of pale surrender. No longer the fearsome crowing of the Great Black Goat. No longer the war cry of the Leader of the Barbey.

Sobharthan stood over the fire. She knew that there was more to come. She knew, if the vision was to be completed, it could not end like this. She watched as the Ram's body, Darkon, burned before her eyes. It burned until there was nothing left except the head. Though it sat amongst the flames, the head had remained unaffected by the fire.

Then the final change began. The features of the head shimmered in the intensity of the white heat, seeming, at first, to melt, as if to follow the way of the body that had gone before it. Then it re-emerged, bearing the features of a *cailleach*, a hag. Rising from the embers, the fully formed body of the *cailleach* stood in front of Sobharthan, daring her with her eyes. The eyes of the Goat, the eyes of Darkon. Good on Evil and Evil on Good. There could be no victor.

The hag moved out from the fire and advanced to the high ground beyond the settlement. She took the corner of her cloak, surveyed the settlement to every side and then, turning in a circle, spread the shadow of the cloak in all directions. The hissing of the water came first; then pools began to form where there was unevenness in the ground. Soon the settlement was

filled with water; the bodies of the dead floated, like
jetsam, on its surface and the skins and hides, that
once were covers on the huts, were strewn across the
wetness. The settlement filled up with water until a
lake had fully formed.

For several moments all was still. Then, a long,
gurgling sound rolled in the bowels of the earth, deep
down beneath the water. Suddenly, much more
quickly than it had appeared, the water emptied from
the lake, leaving no signs whatsoever of the battle that
was fought or of the settlement of Loch Reasc. Neither
the hag nor Sobharthan were anywhere to be seen.

As all assumed a normal state again, a wide grey
image spread itself and glided through the half-light,
descending on the limestone ledge above Loch Reasc.
It closed its wings then, content to stand and look
upon the rich green pasture where once Emlik and his
people had come to settle.

EPILOGUE

All is still. It is morning over Loch Reasc. A thinning mist sits above the place, silvered in the early morning sun. Beneath the dewy gauze, the green and fertile pasture lies, dotted here and there by some wild pigs who have come in search of richer grazing.

On the ledge above the pasture a heron sits, surveying all about him. He looks beyond the pasture. Reflected in his eyes, the green and purple of the distant fern and heather boast their beauty; they have flourished where their seeds have come to lie.

Behind, the greyness of the Burren lightens with the sun, the rock becoming almost white where Moneen meets Aillwee. From their tops the blueness of the ocean can be seen. She is at peace now, the Ocean; her anger resting. Somewhere beyond the quell her waves may thunder, tossing those who have dared to trust her high upon her surf.

The heron spreads his wings now and effortlessly eases himself off of the ledge. The long, loping movement takes him lazily across the pasture. He flies at little height, gliding beneath the flimsy veil of moisture that is yielding to the sun, and comes to rest upon a rock amidst the heather and the fern. He is at home here. He is the watcher of this land.

The heron's eye sees in all directions. It is of the Circle, without beginning and without end. He is the *Seer of Loch Reasc*. Inside, his eyes are filled with Goodness and with Light. When he is gone, the light will seek another eye to watch upon Loch Reasc.

And there will be no end . . .

Hooked
by
Ré Ó Laighléis

Already a 1996 national Oireachtas award-winning novel and shortlisted for the 1997 Bisto Book of the Year Award in its original Irish language form *Gafa*, this book tells the gruelling tale of teenager Alan's slide into the world of drug addiction and his involvement with the murky and danger-filled underworld of same. *Hooked* also relates the parents' story: Sandra's world is thrown into turmoil, first by the realisation that her seventeen-year-old son is in the throes of heroin addiction and then by the discovery of her husband's infidelity. There are no ribbons wrapped around the story here: it is hard, factual and written with sensitivity and skill.

"*Ó Laighléis deftly walks that path between the fields of teenage and adult literature, resulting in a book that will have wide appeal for both young and older readers.*"

Paddy Kehoe, *RTÉ Guide*

"*It paints a graphic picture of a teenager's slide into the world of drugs.*"

Maxine Jones, *The Sunday Tribune*